CORRAL CANYON

CORRAL CANYON

GEORGE FLYNN

A Black Horse Western

ROBERT HALE · LONDON

ISBN 0 7090 5450 5

Robert Hale Limited
Clerkenwell House
Clerkenwell Green
London EC1R 0HT

Photoset in North Wales by
Derek Doyle & Associates, Mold, Clwyd.
Printed and bound in Great Britain by
WBC Ltd, Bridgend, Mid-Glamorgan.

1

A Matter of Judgment

In several thousand miles of mountains, canyons, arroyos, areas of tumbled house-sized prehistoric rock, as well as watercourses which flowed westerly instead of eastward because they were on the wrong side of the Great Divide, it was inevitable that in some places the ancient upheavals would have created bizarre landscapes, such as the one known as Corral Canyon.

It was about forty acres in size. The walls were nearly perpendicular on all sides to a height of roughly two hundred feet. Lizards might be able to climb out but nothing else would be able to.

The only way in and out of Corral Canyon was to the north where whatever upheaval which had created the place, had not done as thorough a job. Both southern walls, where they came around in a rough circle, tapered off in the centre. At one time the boulders which had broken away cluttered the natural entrance.

It was anyone's guess how those immense, enormously heavy blocks of granite had been moved clear to un-block the entrance, but they had.

The only glimmer how this had been accomplished was near the encircling back walls of the canyon where several trees grew close to a fresh-water spring. Back there, once there had been some kind of mud structures, perhaps built by a prehistoric people, possibly the forerunners of Rocky Mountain Indians. How they could have moved boulders as large as a house, was a mystery, but some*one* or some*thing* had rolled the stones on each side of the opening, which was about twenty feet wide with prehistoric sharp edges smoothed over the millennia.

It was one of those places people passed and re-passed without finding. Atop the surrounding top-outs a person could look almost straight down into what would appear to be a very large, grassy bowl. If explorers or travellers had ever done that, there was no indication of their passing. Certainly, every sign pointed to the secret isolation of the huge bowl of a canyon with its nearly straight rock walls rising to a respectable height, with grass stirrup-high covering most of the canyon's floor.

There was an assortment of birds who lived amid the adobe ruins, among the treetops around the spring, and even in parts of the cliff face where holes appeared.

Passing through the wide opening which faced north, a person had the distinct and somewhat uneasy feeling they had passed through time back to eras before mankind. It was silent in the canyon, wind rarely reached there, days and nights and seasons, came and went as inexorably as the passage of time.

It was an ageless as well as timeless place, a secret bowl created while the world had still been hot, which had survived unaltered through millennia of the kind of turbulence which had fashioned the world.

It was one of those places in the immense Rocky chain where prehistory had endured unchanged into modern times. A genuine secret place.

Except for one thing, and the man atop the tired bay horse who rode in past the side-lined big boulders, noticed the inward-swinging old pole gate built of logs and held back by a large stone at its base.

But it was close to dusk when the horseman entered Corral Canyon. By the time he got back to the trees, the spring and what little remained of the mud structure, darkness was settling in.

Even if he'd wanted to go exploring, oncoming darkness and his bone-deep weariness would have combined to induce him to off-saddle near the trees and beside the spring. After hobbling his equally as tired horse, he cleared away twigs and rocks, unfurled his blanket-roll and kicked out of his boots. He drank at the spring, washed his face, lay back on the blanket and rolled a smoke as night arrived.

He was not young, there was grey at his temples, but he lacked a lot of being old. In height and breadth he was average. His clothing was faded, his boots cracked and thin-soled. He talked to the horse, which was cropping grass as though he hadn't eaten in a long time, which he hadn't and had the tucked-up look to prove it.

Accustomed to being talked to and without any

idea what the words meant, the bay horse cropped grass as though he were deaf.

They made a good pair, both were gaunt, weary, and pleased to have followed deer or wapiti trails to this hidden place. The bay horse wasn't smooth-mouthed but neither was he a colt. Like the man, he was living through his prime years. Also, like a man he had signs of having come a considerable distance without much rest. He was short-backed and muscled up. His forelegs were twice as thick as those of most horses and while his shoes were worn almost to the point of dropping off, the horse moved with the suppleness of younger animals.

The spring made the only sound. In fact it hastened slumber for the man lying atop his blankets. He only awakened when the late-night chill arrived, burrowed under the blankets and went back to sleep. It had been several days since he'd slept and he was a hard-sleeper by nature.

Some time in the late night the horse threw up its head and stood like a statue looking back in the direction of the gated opening. He didn't make a sound, but stood like that, ears forward, head high, sorting scents of what he could not identify by sight.

The sun had always belatedly reached into the secret bowl. The man, whose lifelong habit had been to arise before dawn, slept on, even when the birds awakened in their tree tops and began arguing or whatever made birds get noisy as soon as a new day arrived.

The sun came over the high canyon walls. It was high enough when it did this to make the man squint both eyes as he eventually awakened.

For almost a full minute he sat there after pulling on his boots testing the air like a bird dog, before getting to his feet, buckling the hardware in its old worn holster around his middle and going to the creek to complete the awakening process with cold water. The bay horse had already tanked up and was grazing a few yards away. The man rocked back on his heels with a wrinkled nose. The scent he detected was familiar. He arose, turned and saw them, eight or ten of them, apparently waiting for the man to leave the spring so they could drink. Red-backed cattle, tucked up even after grazing all night. Horned cattle, but stolid where they stood watching the man. They had been bred-up until no longhorn showed. They were new-age white-faces, the variety particular stockmen raised for beef, not like razorback longhorns who could out-run a horse and fight a bear to a standstill.

The man went back over among the trees and watched the cattle approach water while keeping a wary eye on the man.

They had two brands, one beside the other. The older scar read as quarter-circle – or horseshoe – R. The other mark was a road brand, the kind drovers marked their stock with when they started a drive. It was simply an oval with a slash through it. Not all trail drivers road-marked cattle, but those who did rarely had arguments with stockmen whose ranges they passed through. Road brands were obvious for what they were, marks put on already-branded cattle to denote a drover's ownership.

The man watched those beeves give his grazing

horse a wide berth, and guessed the reason: They had been driven hard by riders with heavy quirts. The horse did not even look up at the cattle. He knew what they were, had known since, as a three-year-old, the man had taught him to hold the slack on a roped animal.

Gradually other cattle came to the spring. By mid-day they had stuffed one of their stomachs with grass, had filled up with water and scattered out to lie in torpid satisfaction chewing cuds and dozing.

The man made his meagre meal, scoured his fry-pan with grass and as the sun climbed did something he hadn't been able to do in a month, took an all-over bath at the spring, lie flat out atop the blankets and sleep.

When he awakened the sun was gone but not its slanting daylight, got dressed and left the horse, who was dozing in tree-shade, to walk across the meadow to its opening, and to stand there gazing at the closed log gate with a chain securing it.

He climbed through, studied the ground for a while, then went to sit on a rock. The cattle had been driven; after the last cloven-hoof tracks passed into the bowl, there were boot prints where someone had dismounted and closed the gate. There were also shod horse marks. It was difficult to count them in the area of the gate, they crossed and re-crossed, so the man went back down the trail to a narrow place and counted shod horse marks going north, away from the huge natural corral with cattle in it now which hadn't been in it the evening before.

It was quite a hike back for someone who

believed four feet were better than two. He was
sweating by the time he reached the trees and his
blanket roll.

He made a smoke, leaned in tree shade and
made a mental sketch of what he was corralled
with. About sixty-five up-bred white faced cattle
wearing an owner's brand and a road brand.

Those cattle hadn't found this secret place by
themselves, and whoever had driven them had
not only known about the hidden canyon but had
experience driving cattle at night, no small
accomplishment especially when the cattle did
not know the country.

He stubbed out the smoke: Cattle thieves as
surely as hell was hot and – they would be back.
In daylight a point rider would have seen his
tracks entering the hidden canyon. If they
returned today, providing they were good at
reading tracks, they still might pick up his sign,
although with cattle having been driven over
them, it was not likely. Not impossible but
unlikely.

Regardless, he had to get away from here and
not waste a lot of time doing it. He had counted
four sets of shod horse tracks.

He didn't exactly dawdle, but the secret canyon
was more than he could have hoped to find. It was
pleasant, secluded, and had a sweet-water spring.
Last night he had thought he would stay in this
place until both he and the bay horse recovered
from fatigue, and maybe recover a few of the
pounds they had lost getting here.

He did not like interrupting the bay horse's
expectation of rest and good feed. He was fond of

his horse, had bought it as a colt and had never been disappointed in it.

He rolled another smoke with the sun standing overhead. It was hot in the bowl, hot enough for a relaxed human being to doze off after his smoke into a deep, serene and undisturbed sleep right up to the moment someone kicked his boot sole, hard.

There were two of them, bearded, unkempt, unsmiling and expressionless as the awakened man rubbed both eyes, blinked a couple of times and thought fast.

He hadn't meant to sleep, and he certainly had not expected to still be in the box canyon when the drovers who had put the cattle in there, returned.

Neither of the cold-eyed strangers spoke. They had already made their judgment. Whoever the sleeper was, he had been in the canyon far back near the spring last night before the beef had been brought up here. Also, from appearances, the sleeper had been on a long trail, and was a stockman.

The nearest bearded man who was built like a bull, finally spoke as he tossed a six-gun on the blanket roll. 'It's unloaded. Stand up. Who are you and what are you doing in here?'

Standing up was easy but being unarmed was like being naked.

The bay horse had been aroused by the harsh voice. He watched the men by the spring as his owner said, 'My name's Al Castle. I come on to this place just shy of dusk last night. That's a good spring; I figured to lie over a few days until my animal got the pleats out; just loaf an' rest for a spell.'

The other bearded man, as tall but thirty pounds less in heft though just as faded and rough-looking held something out as he said, 'It was in your saddlebags. Partner, you sleep like the dead.'

Al Castle looked at the piece of coarse paper that was being held toward him, and sighed. Whiskers, the burly, unpleasant man, spoke sarcastically. 'Only a damn fool gives his right name when it's on a Wanted dodger ... Two hunnert dollars ain't much of a reward ... What'd you do?'

Al Castle spoke candidly. 'Stole four head of horses.'

'Where?'

'Montana, down near the Wyoming line.'

The man holding the Wanted poster tossed it aside, looked at his companion and waited. It was a short wait. The burly man eyed Castle coldly. 'You done a damn foolish thing, mister, ridin' into this canyon.'

Castle answered while looking steadily at the burly man whose bear-trap mouth was nearly hidden by beard. 'What I done wrong, mister, was steal four horses. If I'd thought on it I'd have stolen cattle.'

The burly man's lips flattened. 'You tryin' to be funny?' Before Castle could answer the speaker jerked his head in the direction of his companion. 'Get his horse. He'll roll the blankets.' As the second man went after the horse the burly man hooked both thumbs in his shellbelt and gently wagged his head. 'Down on your knees; roll that bedroll. Put the gun in your holster leave the bullets where they're lyin'.'

Al Castle knelt and rolled his blankets. He did

not holster the empty six-gun until he was ready
to stand up facing the burly man. 'I don't give a
damn about these cattle,' he said.

The burly man's lips slackened slightly but his
cold eyes remained fixed and hostile. 'Why should
you care about 'em?'

'Because they got a road brand; my guess is that
someone cut them off a drive and brought them up
here until the trail drive was a long way off.'

The burly man's eyes narrowed slightly. 'You're
right, you should have stole cattle. Four horses
ain't worth havin' to ride your butt raw.' He shot a
quick glance at his companion who had led the
horse up. 'Get astride,' the burly man said. 'Tie
your bedroll, mister, ride down to the gate, let
yourself out and chain it closed. You understand?'

Castle nodded and went to test the cinch, which
was snug enough, returned without a word for his
bedroll. He tied it into place from the left side of
the horse. The pair of bearded men were on the
right side. When he was ready to mount he led the
horse out several feet and spoke as he prepared to
swing up across leather.

'As far as I'm concerned, gents, I never found
this corral canyon, never saw no cattle an' never
saw the pair of you.'

The bearded men stood like statues as Al
mounted, evened up his reins and started across
the open land in the direction of the gate.

He wasn't very far when the burly man lifted
out his Colt and slowly raised it. 'He's right about
one thing, Jube. He never seen us an' never found
the canyon.'

Al Castle was slouching in the saddle, both

hands in front. With a sudden twist he swung to look back and fired twice from his freshly loaded hand gun, rocked with the startled bay horse when it shied, got it stopped and shucked out spent casings, replaced them from his belt, leathered the Colt and with both hands atop the saddlehorn, sat there in pleasant sunshine looking back.

The gunshots had scattered cattle in all directions. The pair of animals the bearded men had ridden broke away, stirrups flapping, tails in the air like scorpions, heading back the way they had come as far as the closed gate.

The birds flung skyward in all directions from back by the spring as Al Castle squeezed his horse over into a walk, and rode back almost to the spring before he dismounted and approached the men on the ground, used a boot toe to rock the burly one over on to his back. The bullet had struck him in the middle of the chest. He had been dead before he hit the ground.

The second one was still alive, but just barely. He was leaking blood like a stuck hog. The bullet which had downed him had torn through his right side leaving a ragged strip of flesh hanging amid the filthy, torn shirt.

Castle stood looking down. The bearded man's eyes were wide open, his lips moved but no words came. He made one effort to push up off the ground, fell back and died.

2

Tracks and Trails

When he got down to the gate the rider-less horses were faunching and wide eyed. He dismounted, opened the gate, waited until the terrified horses ran through, led his own animal out and did as the burly man had said, he chained the gate closed.

It was easy to follow the tracks of the stampeded horses of those dead men back in the canyon. He trailed them down to a patch of open country where tall grass waved. The rider-less horses were out there grazing. Terror rarely lasted long with horses.

He made no attempt to get them moving back the way they had come because it was unlikely that they would lead him to wherever they had come from. He circled wide around so as not to disturb them, rode back and quartered; it wasn't difficult to find horse tracks in the tall grass.

He picked up the trail and rode down it without haste. The day was warm, there was the faint fragrance of wild flowers, he rolled and lighted a smoke with both reins looped. When he picked them up he left plenty of slack. His horse might not be able to read tracks but it could go a long way following a scent.

It was a lot longer ride than Castle expected it to be. Not until the rough, high and ragged mountains were behind him and undulating rolls of grassland were ahead under a sky as blue and cloudless as any on earth, did he pick up tracks again, this time in softer ground. Two riders, side by side, heading into the uplands.

He got a surprise when the sun was slanting away and he topped out on a grassy, high roll that ran east and west. About a mile ahead were log buildings, round pole corrals, shade trees big enough to indicate that the ranch up ahead was an old one.

The sign led directly toward the buildings. Castle turned eastward, approached the yard from that direction and was greeted by barking dogs while he was still a half mile from the yard.

Watch dogs inevitably brought people. Castle studied them riding at a dead walk. There was a woman, and three men, unshaven men, wearing shellbelts and sidearms, something working cattlemen rarely did. Hand weapons and their accoutrements got in the way of men labouring by hand or from horseback.

He passed two large old unkempt trees when someone on the porch snarled at the dogs. They slunk back closer to the house. Castle saw one of the men lean slightly and say something to the other men.

He halted at the tie-rack over in front of a huge log barn instead of crossing to the house and dismounting over there. One of the men came down off the porch and walked with a strong stride in the direction of the barn. He wasn't young and he wasn't smiling when he halted near the far end of the tie-rack and said, 'Good day.'

Castle gauged the man. He was thick and powerful. His holster was low with the tie-down across the grips. Castle smiled and returned the greeting. 'G'day. I seen the buildings an' wondered if you folks needed a hired hand.'

The unsmiling man turned and called. 'Do we need a hired hand?'

The elder of the men on the porch answered shortly. 'No we don't.'

The man facing Castle shrugged. 'Paw says we don't … But I heard a few days back old man Black's hiring.' The man raised his arm. 'East of here maybe three, four miles. His name's Elijah Black. He adjoins us easterly and northerly … Cantankerous old devil, but he'd be your best bet.' Finally, the big man smiled. 'Good luck. This time of year someone'll be hiring.'

Al Castle unlooped his reins, turned the horse once and swung into the saddle. He smiled. 'Much obliged. Mind if I ask your name?'

'Don't mind at all. My name's Pete. The fellers yonder are my paw, the grey-headed one: Amos Humphrey. The feller beside him is my brother Martin. Martin Humphrey.'

Castle was obliged to return the courtesy. He did not avoid using his own name, he had forgotten the dodger back in the canyon, and didn't bat an eye as he said. 'Al Castle. Well, I'll go try Mister Black. I'm right obliged.'

He rode out of the yard heading eastward. He did not look back; they would be watching. When he was a mile along he tried to make up his mind if the dead men in the canyon resembled the live ones he'd just left. Size and heft were about right, but beards ruled out any compatible comparison. Whether those two up yonder were related or not, they sure-Lord had come from the Humphrey yard. He had tracked them that far without much difficulty.

He didn't find the Black outfit because he encountered a town before he got that far along. As he turned southward on the roadway he saw the bullet-riddled sign about four or five hundred yards out that said Campton. Population 600. Beneath someone had scribbled with chalk: Counting dogs and headstones.

It was a pleasant-appearing town with shade trees, a broad roadway and stores opposite each other. The livery barn was near the centre of town, which was unusual. Usually businesses like tan yards and livery barns were at the lower end.

There was a mercantile with oiled floors, a land office, a harness works, a log jailhouse, a pool hall and several other businesses. The saloon was near the upper end of Campton.

When Castle walked in beating off dust only two men looked up. One was a rawboned older man with steel-blue eyes and a gimpy leg that showed only when he moved. He nodded at Castle.

The other man was about as average as was Castle. He was dressed in the same faded rangeman's attire and except for a big drooping dragoon moustache and a dull-shiny marshal's badge on his shirt, could have passed for any run-of-the-mill rider.

Castle settled against the bar. 'Beer,' he told the barman, and saw the limp as soon as the tall, rawboned man turned.

The marshal said, 'Musket ball in an In'ian fight when he was a youngster.' The marshal shoved out a hand. 'Tom Waters, Town Marshal.'

Castle gripped and released the hand. 'Al Castle.'

Several blue-tailed flies were beating themselves against a dirty front window and two old men shuffled in, nodded to the barman and took chairs near the stove which was not lighted, rarely was this time of year, and relaxed.

Castle offered a slight salute to the barman and his friend, half emptied his glass, put it down and fished for the makings. 'How far from here is the Black outfit?' he asked before lighting up.

'The headquarters is no more'n maybe a mile easterly. You can't miss it … Did the old man send for you?' the marshal asked.

'No. Some fellers named Humphrey said they thought Mister Black was hiring.'

The two older men exchanged a glance. The marshal drained his beer glass. The barman seemed on the point of speaking but didn't. Not until Al remarked casually that the Humphreys had told him old man Black was a cougar to work for, and that remark encouraged the barman.

'He's an old son of a bitch. If he hires you, you'll find out. His missus died six, seven years back.'

The marshal interrupted to say, 'Eight years, Jeb.'

The barman nodded curtly. 'Eight years ago. He wasn't real pleasant before that ... Afterwards ... Well, Mister Castle I don't doubt but that he'll hire you. He's always got a place for a new hand. He don't keep hired men more'n a month or two.'

Marshal Waters considered his empty glass until the barman understood and limped away to refill it. Waters said, 'Partner, there's other outfits. This time of year some must still be hiring. If you work for old Elijah too long, about the time he fires you the other outfits'll have all the men they need.'

The marshal gave Castle the names of several other cow outfits along with directions how to find them.

It was the rawboned unsmiling barman who caught and held Castle's attention when he said, 'The old devil's hired and fired no less'n five men since hiring season begun. The last time he was in here he got about half drunk an' told me they don't have rangemen like they had when he was young. He said two men got hurt at the markin' ground; one of 'em got the iron knocked back by an old cow, and the feller branded his foot. The old man laughed an' said that was the only man he'd ever hired that wore a quarter circle R on his boot.'

Castle dawdled, made a cigarette, emptied his glass, considered his itchy face in the backbar mirror, went up to the tonsorial parlour for a shave and a shearing, and had no difficulty at all getting the barber to talk. When Castle mentioned quarter circle R it was like pulling the plug of a dam. Even after he was finished and had

been paid two bits, the barber still recalled anec-
dotes, rumours, all kind of colourful local gossip
about Elijah Black.

Castle ate at the cafe where he was just another
nondescript rangeman, not quite ignored by the
cafeman but not heeded as the cafeman carried on a
running conversation with two men in matching
britches and coats, wearing ties around their necks.
He had always been impressed by indications of
affluence, but he had never learned to differentiate
between genuine men of substance and travelling
drummers who also dressed to the nines without
having a second cent to bless themselves with.
Castle considered the sky out front. The day was
wearing along. He considered bedding down in
Campton and only decided against it when Town
Marshal Waters came by, paused and said, 'Only
about a mile. If he don't hire you on, you can make it
back here to the rooming house before dark.'

It was a friendly town, no different from hun-
dreds like it between the Missouri River and the
Sierra Nevadas. Castle accepted the lawman's
suggestion; as he rode toward the only visible set of
large buildings in the fading day, he even specu-
lated about settling in the Campton country. He'd
never really had a home. Since his early teens
when his father, mother and two uncles died
during an epidemic, Al Castle had been on his own.
He had a deep-down longing to belong, to be part of
something.

When he entered Elijah Black's yard a furious
argument was in progress over on the porch of the
main-house. A grizzled old man was shouting at a
much taller, heavier and younger dark man.

Neither one heeded the horseman who tied up in front of the barn, or to the pair of rangemen standing like stones under the small overhang of the bunkhouse.

They were so angry, so near to fighting, that if the Angel Gabriel had floated into the yard playing a yard long golden trumpet it was doubtful if either man on the porch would have spared him a glance.

Castle went as far as the bunkhouse porch. Only one of the riders turned, and immediately turned back. The argument on the porch was getting close to the point where one or the other of the angry men would get violent.

Castle asked what the ruckus was about, and was again ignored. Under the circumstances most men would not have set a foot off the bunkhouse porch, but Castle did after being ignored by the stationary men under the overhang.

He sauntered to the wide steps leading to the porch and mildly asked where he could find Mister Black. Again, he was ignored. The burly, large dark man was bringing up a fist. He didn't move fast. The old man stepped back as he venomously said, 'You raise a hand to me an' I'll blow your damned head off!'

The dark man lowered his fist. The old man was out of reach. He opened the hand and it hovered above the holstered Colt when Castle spoke again in the same mild tone of voice, but this time he spoke into a lull while the angry men on the porch paused to catch their breath. He addressed the large dark man.

'Leave it be, mister.'

For the first time the angry rangeman turned to face what he perceived as a nondescript individual. He snarled at Castle. 'Keep your gawddamned nose out of this – you son of a bitch!'

Castle freed his tie-down thong. 'Draw!' he said. Every spectator including the furious old man with awry grey hair and beard-stubbed face stopped moving. Under the bunkhouse overhang the two rangemen scarcely breathed.

Castle spoke again without batting an eye, addressing the large man on the porch. 'I don't care what your squabble's about, but I don't like bein' swore at … Go ahead, *do it*!'

The old man snorted. 'Well Dowd, what you waitin' for?'

The large man flashed for his six-gun but he was facing the old man whose taunt had been the last of many. Castle shot without seeming to have moved. His bullet hit the holstered gun, tore the holster loose and impact swung the large man sideways where he fought desperately for balance before striking the log wall and falling. His six-gun skittered off the porch.

The old man froze in place. He no longer looked angry, just awed. Across the yard one of the onlookers at the bunkhouse turned to the other. 'Did he hit him?'

'No,' his companion replied. 'At least I don't think so, but he sure as hell shot the holster before Dowd could draw … Who is he?'

'How would I know, he just rode into the yard. That's his bay horse at the rack.'

'We better go see how bad Dowd is hurt.'

'Not on your life. We stay right here. Let the old

man look to Dowd.'

The old man did, but the moment he saw the damage and what had been accomplished, he stood above the injured man gloating. 'Serve you right, you dang half-breed pup. Get up, get your things out of the bunkhouse and don't even look back. *Get up!*'

Dowd didn't get up, he tried and fell back. The old man gloated. 'Your hip's broke. Crawl if you can't walk; be out of my yard within.....'

Castle interrupted still speaking softly. 'Help him up.'

The old man turned with bared teeth. 'He can rot where he's lyin' ... Who the hell you think you are comin' on to my land an' orderin' me around!'

Castle holstered his weapon, went up the steps, caught hold of the old man by the scruff and propelled him with a hard shove toward the downed man. 'Help him up! Mister, I'm not like him, I don't argue. *Help him up!*'

The old man glared and sputtered right up until Castle hit him in the chest. He went down unhurt but wild-eyed angry. As he got back to his feet, 'I'll kill you, you son.....'

'Be careful, Mister Black. If you finish that you'll carry your guts into the house in a bucket. For the last time – *help him up!*'

The old man's mouth was a bloodless slit, his body was tensed forward, Castle nodded at him. 'Go ahead. You're too old to use a gun, but go ahead.'

It was Dowd arising with the aid of the log wall at his back who spoke behind the old man. 'You don't stand the chance of a snowball in hell,

Mister Black ... I was fixin' to gut-shoot you. Go ahead, choose him.'

Too much time had passed, the old man was still orry-eyed angry, but in the back of his mind silent warning bells were sounding. He came upright slowly, right hand clear of the hip-holster. 'Who the hell do you think you are?' he blustered. Even the onlookers at the bunkhouse relaxed. There would be no killing. The old man's voice had sounded garrulous, not furious.

'My name's Al Castle. You'll be Mister Black. I was told in town you might be hiring.'

'You!' the old man exclaimed. 'Me hire you! Get on your horse, get off my land an' if I ever see you on it again......'

'You're too old, Mister Black. An' I got eyes in the back of my head.'

Castle shouldered the old man aside, helped Dowd off the wall and used an arm around Dowd's middle to get him down off the porch. As they were crossing toward the bunkhouse Dowd said, 'What'd you butt in for? I'd have killed the old bastard.'

'Maybe he's an old bastard, but he's too old. If the law didn't call it murder other folks would.'

Castle handed the man with the sore hip to the pair of sober-faced men on the bunkhouse porch, went to the barn to put up his horse and care for it, and eventually emerged to roll and light a smoke. There was a single bright light at the main-house. Old man Black was pouring himself a half water-glass full of whiskey. He was still mad.

3
Old Elijah

When Castle was outside the following morning helping one of the riders do the chores, the old man appeared in the barn. Whether he had thought the stranger had left the following night or not, he looked genuinely surprised to see him and one of his hired men, the one named Morris, doing the chores and casually talking. He got red in the face, stamped over where Al Castle was forking hay to stalled horses, planted his legs wide and with both hands on his hips, said, 'I told you last night to get off my land. You deef?'

Al put the three-tined fork aside, gazed at the old man who hadn't shaved and in other ways looked as unkempt as some old widowers became, and smiled. 'I work for you, Mister Black. You remember?'

'Remember what!'

'You hired me last night.'

The other rider was leaning on his manure fork watching and listening. His eyes widened at what Castle had said. So did the old man's eyes. He stared and frowned. For a moment he seemed unsure. He turned to Morris. 'Did I say anythin' about hirin' this feller?' he asked. Morris solemnly nodded his head.

Old man Black faced Castle again, pondered briefly before getting in the last word. 'Then what'n hell you doin' leanin' on the fork? Get to work.' The old man went as far as the barn's doorless front opening, then paused and turned.

'Where's Dowd?'

Morris was still leaning on the manure fork watching the old man when he replied. 'Gone. Saddled up and left before sunup.'

Elijah slowly smiled. 'Didn't get the wages comin' to him,' he said and continued on his way toward the main-house.

Morris looked at Castle, shook his head resignedly and went back to dunging out stalls. He and Castle were still choring when the other Quarter Circle R rider came into the barn. He was a beanpole of a man, tall, ageless and already with a cud in his cheek. He watched Castle for a moment then asked Morris what the old man had wanted. Morris told him of the bald lie with a straight face.

The thin tall man spat then laughed. Castle and Morris smiled too. Castle asked them how old Elijah Black was. Neither of them knew. The beanpole, whose name was Avery, dryly commented, 'I doubt if he knows himself.'

Castle was interested. 'How long you worked for him?'

'Before his missus died, must be maybe ten years.'

Castle considered the tall man. 'What I heard in

town he don't keep hired hands more'n a few months.'

Avery nodded about that as he said, 'I'm his brother-in-law. His wife was my sister.' As though that explained everything Avery moved to help with the chores.

The following morning when the three of them were dawdling because Elijah hadn't come from the house to give them instructions for the day, Avery looked at Castle and shrugged. 'Times he's not as ornery as other times,' he said.

Morris made a comment about that. 'When he's been drinkin' he's bearable.'

The sun was high with the riders still loafing at the bunkhouse. Morris and Avery became uneasy. Avery finally said, 'Probably passed out last night. He's been drinkin' more'n more.' Avery left the bunkhouse heading for the main-house. He wasn't gone fifteen minutes and returned looking worried. 'He's still in bed. Something's wrong. He looked right at me an' didn't say a word. He sort of writhed under the covers.'

Morris gazed steadily at the thin man. 'Want me to go to Campton for Doc Simpson?'

Avery nodded, went to a bench at the long bunkhouse table and sat down. 'I expect one of us ought to, Morris … He … He's alive an' all but something's wrong. I don't think he can talk.'

Morris left heading for one of the horses in a pole corral behind the barn. Avery and Castle were still sitting in the bunkhouse when they heard Morris leave the yard on horseback.

The tall, thin man sat as though he was stunned. After a long while he began to speak.

'I've know Elijah a long time. Him an' my sister was like two peas in a pod. I don't know what's wrong with him.'

Castle rolled and lighted a smoke as he said, 'How do you put up with him?'

'Well ... when my sister was dyin' she asked me to look after him.'

'You said you would?'

'Yes ... He was different back then; not easy or anythin' like that, but a lot better'n he become after she died.' Avery looked at Castle wearing a sad little smile. 'Old bastard's fired me every Friday for ten years.'

Castle watched blue smoke trickling. 'You like him, Avery?'

The tall man seemed to have to consider that. He didn't answer for a spell. Eventually he said, 'Years back, yes. We got along. Had dis-agreements but we got along ...'

'You still like him?'

' ... Your name is Castle?'

'Yes. Al Castle.'

' ... Al. I give my word to my sister.'

Castle went outside onto the little covered porch, sank into a battered chair and did not move until Avery came out and joined him, then Castle asked a question. 'Has Quarter Circle R sold cattle lately?'

Avery was gravely looking in the direction of the main-house when he answered. 'Yes. Three hundred head. Prime beef.'

'To a road-drover?'

Avery turned. 'Yes. What made you ask?'

It was Castle's turn to hang fire over an answer.

'Figured it might be. This time of year they can graze along, buy a few head here'n there on their way to a shipping point.'

The answer seemed to satisfy the thin, tall man. He had other things on his mind. They sat out there like mutes until Al saw a pair of hastening riders and pointed. Avery stood up. He recognised the man riding with Morris and said, 'Doc Simpson. I hope he ain't too late.'

The medical doctor was a grizzled man with shrewd eyes and wrinkled matching coat and britches. He had a little leather satchel tied to the saddle which he removed as he dismounted and Morris took the reins to his horse. The medical man nodded to Avery and Castle. He clearly knew Avery. 'Where is he – in the house?'

'Yes. He don't ....'

'Come along,' growled the grizzled man and struck off across the yard. The only sound until Morris returned from the barn was a door slamming at the main-house. Al asked if the doctor had said anything on the ride from town. Morris eased down into the vacated chair. 'He's a closed-mouth old screwt. His disposition ain't much different from Elijah's only he controls it better ... No, he didn't say much, just that Elijah has been under a guardian angel for a long time; an' the guardian angel must've got tired of helpin' a man who won't help hisself.'

Castle shoved his legs out, hooked his boots over the little railing and tipped down his hat. It was pleasantly cool under the overhang. Given a chance he would have dozed. Instead he gazed far out with narrowed eyes right up until the doctor

came marching back toward the barn without
Avery. He stopped to gaze at the seated men. 'He
had a little stroke, the damned old screwt. Drinks,
eats when he wants to, drinks too much ... He's
had high blood pressure for years. Talkin' sense to
him is like reasonin' with an old mammy cow ...
I'll see if the nurse will come out here, make him
eat right, quit whiskey, and for gosh sakes take an
all over bath.'

Morris went to the barn to lend a hand with the
doctor's horse, when he returned and sat with Al
Castle watching the rumpled physician squaw-
reining back in the direction of town, he said, 'I
can't stand too much of this settin'. You like to
ride out a ways? Avery'n I was sortin' through
lookin' for first-calf heifers in trouble before this
happened.'

They went to the barn, rigged out and left the
yard in a steady walk. Clearly, Morris's world had
been turned upside down. He was an itinerant
range man, but nothing like this had ever
happened with him before, and the working
season wasn't even half over.

They talked, had an occasional smoke, sifted
through quite a few bands of grazing cattle,
eventually went to a sweet-water spring and
hobbled their animals, squatted in shade of a
huge old black oak tree, and loafed. It was getting
along toward late afternoon.

Morris said, 'The old man's got thousands of
acres. His line runs plumb over to the Humphrey
place an' even farther in other directions ... Too
much land an' too many cattle for just me'n Avery
to look after. The old man rides out now'n again,

but don't stay with us long, heads back for the yard.'

'How many cattle?' Castle asked.

Morris made a gesture. 'Who the hell knows? Short time back the old man sold several hunnert head to a driftin' drover. Me'n Avery picked 'em out, rounded 'em up and delivered 'em to the road-trader in one day, an' there was still cattle like hair on a dog's back.'

Castle considered his scuffed boot toes as he asked a question. 'Is he ever bothered with rustlers?'

Morris's answer was predictable. 'If it happens we got no way of knowin'. Avery told me one time they used to hire five, six riders every season. Him an' me, even when Elijah goes out with us, can't begin to do all that should be done, an' meanwhile the damned bulls keep makin' more calves.'

Morris faced Al Castle in speckled tree shade. 'If the old man's in real bad shape, I don't know what'll happen. I'll go lookin' for another job, but it's late in the season.'

'Did the old man have any children?'

Morris shook his head. 'They couldn't. I got no idea why but Avery told me one time they couldn't have kids. I never asked an' Avery never mentioned it again.' His gaze at Castle narrowed slightly. 'You're wonderin' who'll get the outfit?'

'No. I was just askin' questions.'

'I'd say if Elijah dies Avery will get it. Far as I know he's the only kin.'

As Castle arose and dusted off he had one more question. 'How long you been with the old man?'

'Last year I come in late. He'd just fired a rider

so I got hired on an' finished the season. This spring I come back. He hired me back.'

'Do you like him?'

'Well, that's hard to answer. The three of us'd play poker after supper sometimes. When he'd lose he'd jump up red in the face and cuss a blue streak. After that he'd storm out of the bunkhouse. Avery'n I'd laugh until we nearly cried ... I guess I liked him; it was hard to do sometimes but hell I've worked for a lot of stockmen. Elijah has his likes in other parts of the country.'

Morris sounded like a tolerant, easy-going individual.

They snugged up, got astride and headed for the yard. It would be close to dusk when they got there but they were in no greater hurry going back than they had been going out.

The bunkhouse was cold. Morris got a fire going and went out front to gaze worriedly in the direction of the main-house. When Castle joined him Morris said, 'I don't know what to make of this. Should I go over there or should I wait until Avery comes back?'

Castle had no advice to offer, he sank into one of the porch chairs, propped his feet on the railing and was lost in thought right up to the moment when Morris spoke sounding relieved.

'Avery's comin'.'

The three of them entered the bunkhouse where Avery fiddled with the hanging lamp while Morris fired up the stove for supper. Avery said nothing until Morris produced a hidden bottle and placed it beside Avery on the table. Avery raised the bottle, lowered it, knocked the stopper back into place with his palm and said, 'He had a stroke. You know what that is?'

If either Castle or Morris knew they didn't say, they watched the old man's brother-in-law and waited.

'It's got somethin' to do with your insides. Somethin' occludes – that's Doc Simpson's word – the flow of blood. Somethin' inside bursts, leaves you so's sometimes you can't talk an' maybe can't walk.' Avery paused to raise the bottle again. He resumed speaking as he put it down. 'Doc said he won't be able to tell how bad off Elijah'll be until he comes back in a few days. He said Elijah can't do much without someone to look after him … He said he'd see if he can get Nancy to come out an' look after him until he knows just how serious the stroke is … He said sometimes one stroke'll be followed by another one – and that usually kills a person. Maybe, if it's not much of a stroke a man can recover but he'll never be as good a man as he was before.'

Morris put meat in an iron fry-pan. The smell reminded Castle he hadn't eaten since morning. Avery sat slumped and solemn. When it seemed he had nothing more to say he made one more remark. 'I told him about Elijah an' Dowd havin' a near knock down an' drag out last night on the porch. Doc said that could have triggered it, but he also said Elijah was a walkin' time bomb, what with his disposition an' all, it was bound to happen sooner or later anyway.'

Avery abruptly stood up knocking over the bottle as he did so and stormed out of the

bunkhouse slamming the door hard after himself.
He did not return. Morris and Al Castle ate in
silence. As they were clearing up the dishes
Morris said, 'Strange thing – Avery was fond of
the old bastard. Maybe because he understood
him, maybe because of what he promised his
sister ... I've stood by when old Elijah would cuss
him out enough to make a man shoot the old
bastard. Avery just stood there like he was deaf.
One time I said somethin' to him about that. He
answered without lookin' at me; he said the old
man never got over the death of his wife; didn't
know who to blame so he blamed everybody ...
Does that sound right to you?'

Al Castle was drying dishes with a soggy old
cloth when he answered. 'I got no idea. I know
livestock. That's about all I know ... Tell me
somethin', Morris: When the old man sold them
three hundred critters to the road-drover ... Did
anythin' happen?'

'Happen? Like what?'

'Well; like maybe the drover lost some of them
cattle.'

Morris was drying his hands before lowering his
sleeves when he answered. 'Where did you get
such an idea? No, nothin' happened. Me'n Avery
made the cut, delivered 'em to the drover; he
didn't even stop. He had three Messican cowboys.
They had the herd movin'. The drover counted the
critters, his riders pushed them in with the others
and kept on going. Simple as that ... There wasn't
no trouble at all.'

They went outside for a smoke. Avery was in
one of the chairs like he'd been moulded there.

Castle hunkered with his back to the log wall. Morris took the chair. There were only two chairs.

It was uncomfortable until Avery arose without a word and headed for the main-house, then Morris said, 'I don't envy him, settin' up all night with the old man.'

The following morning Castle and Morris were still adrift when Avery appeared, tired-eyed, unshaven and more gaunt looking than usual. He hardly looked at Castle when he said, 'Might be a good idea to see if there's any bulls at the mud holes.'

Morris nodded, stood with Castle watching the tall man return to the house. Morris shook his head. 'It ain't like him not to say how the old man is. Well hell; let's go see if there's bulls standin' in mud somewhere.'

Over the years Elijah Black had imported pure bred Hereford bulls that came off good grass and soft earth ranges. Bulls with soft feet had to follow bulling cows just as hard as did range-bred bulls, but their feet wore down, got hot, and the bulls would find a spring with mud and stand in it, which would have been all right except that mud-wallow bulls didn't breed cows, so rough-country rangemen had to check for sore-footed bulls and drive them back to cows.

It was one of those chores the old-timers never had to worry about. Elijah had cussed about it. In his youth stockmen raised range bulls and, in order to avoid in-breeding, traded them with other stockmen. In those days a bull was a rough, tough, ornery critter. Elijah scorned those purebred bulls with punky feet, but he wouldn't have gone back to the old slab-sided, long-horned, mean bulls which could clear a six-foot corral fence like a bird and would fight anything, even a man on horseback, which the purebreds would not do.

What Al and Morris found at the third sump-spring was a few cows standing in mud along with the bulls. They drove them all out, avoided one belligerent bull who wanted to fight but was hesitant about tackling mounted men. He would have run them out of the country if they'd been on foot.

The hot season was close. It wasn't quite uncomfortable yet but that would change shortly. The cattle were in good flesh, even the mammy-cows with sassy big calves at their sides. They got careless a couple of times. A cow with a small calf was the cause of more injuries among rangemen than bulls ever were, but well-mounted riders could avoid protective cows without difficulty.

Along toward mid-afternoon they started back. They had cleared six or eight bulls out of mud-holes along with a few cows. Al asked about the range. Morris made a careless wave. 'I don't think the old man knows where his boundary lines are. I sure don't. Hell, he's got deeded country for more miles than you'n I could ride over in a couple of days. Westerly a few miles he borders the Humphreys. They ranch close to rough country.'

Al asked about the Humphreys. Morris was indifferent when he answered. 'There's the old man, two boys an' the girl. The old lady died a few years back.'

'How many cattle do they run?'

'Not many, a few hundred head. They raise a lot of horses. I think the old man likes horses better'n cattle. Sometimes I can't blame him – but in this country a man can starve raisin' horses. Only In'ians eat horse meat.'

'Does Humphrey have hired riders?'

'Two. I don't know where he got 'em. They got beards birds could nest in. Not real neighbourly fellers. Avery'n I run into 'em now an' then when the cattle drift an' get mixed.'

Al Castle said very little more as they saw the buildings ahead. He had been on the Elijah Black place for several days now. Sure as hell someone – the Humphreys most likely – had gone up to corral canyon and found two corpses back near the spring.

Avery was at the bunkhouse when they headed in that direction after caring for their animals. Avery didn't smile but he greeted them like a man in good spirits. Morris related what they had accomplished as Avery stoked the wood-stove and fired the kindling.

Morris got his hidden bottle, drank, handed the bottle to Al, who also swallowed a couple of times and passed the bottle to Avery, who drank, blew out a flammable breath and handed back the bottle as he said, 'Doc come back this morning.'

Morris and Castle sat at the table waiting for Avery to finish fiddling with the fire before he also said, 'He brought Nan. She's goin' to stay a while.'

Morris was more interested in Elijah. 'How's the old man?'

'Well; Nan got him settin' up.'

'Can he talk?'

'Sort of. Can't understand most of it but he can talk. Doc says he's got to stay down for a while.' Avery paused to smile for the first time since last week. 'The old man like to have had a fit. Doc pushed him down in the bed and said if he so much as raised his voice he'd give the nurse something to inject him to knock him out for a month.'

Castle said, 'Sounds promising.'

Avery agreed, dished up two plates and when they stared he said he'd eat at the main-house and departed.

Morris ate like there was to be no tomorrow. Castle ate well too, but he was thoughtful. They had nothing more to say until later, when full night was down and they were outside on the porch chairs.

As Castle built a smoke he asked a question. 'Has there been rustlin' in this country lately?'

Morris trickled smoke as he answered. 'Not that I've heard of. I guess years back there was some. The old man's told us of runnin' thieves down an' leavin' them hanging in trees in their camp. But that was long ago. Far as I know there's been no thievin' in years.'

Al killed his smoke and went inside to bed down. He lay a while with both arms under his head looking at the bottom of the upper bunk before he sighed and closed his eyes.

4
Complications

Castle rode out again with Morris the following day. With good grass, calving mostly over by late springtime, a rangeman's work settled into categories of 'doctoring', killing the predatory varmints that hung on the outskirts of calvy cows, waiting for afterbirth or, if they were bold enough, a new-born, watching for screw-worm infestations and an assortment of other things, such as chasing bulls away from mud holes and helping the occasional first-calf heifer delivery, if she was hung up.

Mostly, it was routine. Not until autumn when a gather was made separating animals, usually big fat two-year-olds and gummer cows or aged bulls, was the work hard and demanding.

As Morris said while they were sifting through the cattle watching for anything likely to be life-threatening, spring and summer were good times of each year; there was sunshine, fragrance, azure skies, easy riding to do and places where men could sit in shade and smoke or nap.

Castle knew all of this. He'd been working

ranges since he'd straddled his first horse. He was more interested in what Morris had to say about Quarter Circle R, its people and the neighbours.

When they finished their wandering and headed for the yard, Al Castle was heading for a surprise that would have far-reaching complications.

They were in the barn caring for their animals when Avery arrived. His mood was even better than it had been the day before. He and Morris carried on a running conversation until the three of them were ready to go over to the bunkhouse, then Avery said, 'Nan's got a real talent with sick folks. She give Elijah an all-over bath.' Avery paused to laugh. 'It took both of us. He fought like a wounded eagle, cussed and hollered. The madder he got the easier it was to understand some of his moods.' Avery eyed Morris. 'You know Nan?'

Morris nodded. 'I know her. I never seen a woman muscled up like a man before. No wonder she ain't married.'

Avery was still smiling when they entered the bunkhouse and he went to feed kindling into the stove and get a fire going. He was still amused as he straightened up. 'He fired her. She looked at me kind of uncertain. I told her he'd been firing me for close to eight, ten years, not to pay him any mind … You know what she done?'

Morris shook his head. Castle did not even do that much. He had no idea who the nurse was.

'She finished dryin' him off, picked him up like he was a baby and tossed him on the bed. You should've seen the old man's face. A man could have straddled one eyeball an' sawed off the other one.'

They ate with Avery still regaling them about old man Black and the nurse. When they finished Avery left to visit the main-house, Morris made a smoke, let it droop as he filled the wash-pan from the stove's reservoir, rolled up his sleeves and said, 'Elijah's too cranky to die, an' that woman's too tough to let him die.' To keep smoke from making his eyes sting he killed the quirley and went to fling the water out back, hang the big pan from its nail and roll down his sleeves.

As he refilled a cup with coffee he said, 'One word of advice. I know this is a lonely life, but if you get to hankerin' after a female go to town, to the saloon or the dance hall. That woman cracked a man's jaw couple of years back for tryin' to kiss her.'

The following morning all three riders were rigging out in the barn when Elijah's nurse appeared in the doorway. She addressed Avery without heeding Castle and Morris. She wanted him to see if he could find a certain kind of tree and fetch back the bark. When she finished speaking she turned, saw Al Castle, turned rigid with both eyes sprung wide.

He recognised her at the same time; the woman on the porch at the Humphrey place. That time he hadn't more than glanced at her but there was no mistaking, it was the same woman, and she was indeed muscularly put together. More so than men expected in female-women.

He nodded. She turned on her heel and went slowly back to the house. Avery and Morris, busy with their animals missed the exchange of stares. Castle led his mount outside with the others to turn it once before stepping over leather. What troubled him most of this day was her reaction. She had recognised him, but there was more to it than that. He could not define the look on her face, it was more than just surprise.

The day was spent like many others this time of year, checking for drift, passing mud holes, sifting through scattered bands of Quarter Circle R cattle, watching for heifers with one tiny hoof protruding where there was supposed to be two.

They killed an hour on a slight rise where white oaks grew, their tops alive with birds. Avery mentioned his relief about the old man. Morris told Avery about warning the new hired hand about Nancy. Avery nodded. 'All the Humphreys is touchy. Except the old lady. She was nice and pleasant.'

They headed for the yard as the sun was changing colour the closer it got to setting. There was smoke coming from the kitchen stovepipe at the main-house. Morris made a wistful remark. 'It'd be nice if she'd come to the bunkhouse an' cook us a real woman-cooked supper. The only thing worse'n eatin' our own cookin' is that Mex cafe in town.'

There was a strange horse at the tie-rack out front of the main-house which provoked curiosity among the riders, but not very much. Elijah wasn't burdened with friends but he had business callers now and then. They didn't bother to go look at the brand. They settled under the overhang – this time Al got the chair and Morris had to hunker against the log wall.

There were lights in the main-house before a large, loose-moving man with a salt-and-pepper beard came out. The watchers at the bunkhouse did not require good visibility to tell that the bearded man was mad. He jerked his reins from the tie-rack, tugged his cinch tight, swung into the saddle and growled at the horse. He left the yard in a lope in the direction of Campton.

Morris made a dry remark. 'Someone put a burr under his saddle blanket.'

The topic was exhausted. Avery mentioned there being something familiar abut the bearded man. Neither Al or Morris took that up.

Later, Avery thought they ought to ride the far northern range tomorrow. There hadn't been riders up there since last winter and while cattle had no reason to climb hills covered with pine and fir needles, there was always the chance some would – and those uplands had mountain lions and bears, creatures that could take down and kill an eight-hundred-pound cow.

In the old days it hadn't been that easy. The slab-sided razorback longhorns of Elijah's youth could, in fair fight and maybe die themselves, kill a lion or a bear, get them down and paw them to mincemeat.

It was a long and fruitless ride but they did find some critters too close to the timbered mountains, and drifted them back a couple of miles. They saw both cougar and bear sign. Morris thought the predators had come almost to the edge of the timber using cattle-scent to guide them. He was of the opinion that Avery'd had a good notion to ride this far.

This time they got back after dark. They could have got back sooner but with no need they hadn't pushed the horses.

Avery went over to the main-house to eat. He came back an hour later, sat at the table looking at Al Castle. 'Did you ever see Nan Humphrey before?' he asked.

'I rode into their yard when I was headin' over this way. They didn't need a hired hand. Why?'

'Well, like I said, it's a little hard to understand Elijah, but he can talk a little better each time I go visit. He told me Nan asked a lot of questions about you.'

Castle thought one thing and said another. *They had found those two dead men!* 'Like I said, I rode into the Humphrey yard. They directed me over here, said Mister Black might be hiring.'

Morris laughed. 'She's interested, Al. It's about time – she's got to be in her twenties.'

Avery took it up from Morris. 'You rode into the yard and rode out. Maybe ... Like Morris said, she's a spinster lady; I've heard they get the hankerin' pretty bad.'

Except for sly remarks about what Morris and Avery thought had the makings of a courtship, the subject was allowed to die. Later, with the bunkhouse dark and snoring men nearby, Al again lay back with both arms under his head wide awake.

Why him? He'd made a big sashay to approach the yard from the east. *Tracks!* He tossed in his soogans. Why hadn't he just kept on riding? But tracks could be made by anyone, maybe not exactly the way he had left his sign, but that wasn't enough to hang a man. A man'd want to be sure of that in new country.

The following morning after cleaning up and shaving he visited Elijah, who did not recognise him right away but who eventually did.

The muscular, handsome woman hovered as they talked. It was hard for Castle to make conversation; he and Elijah weren't that well acquainted. Except for Castle's intervention in the squabble on the porch, they didn't have much in common.

He and the woman exchanged several long glances before Al left the house, went to the barn, found Morris and Avery gone, and snaked out a fresh animal from the corral behind the barn to lead it inside to be saddled, and stopped stone still. The woman was standing midway along with both hands clasped across her middle. She neither smiled nor spoke until Al had tied the horse, then she said, 'Is your name really Castle?'

He smiled at her. 'Yes ma'm. An' yours is Nan Humphrey.'

She ignored his smile and pleasant tone. 'When you came into our yard some time back, you came from the east.'

Al's brain was flashing warning signals. 'Yes'm, but I sashayed around a little first. Them dogs didn't sound friendly. It's always a good idea not to ride right up onto folks.'

'Is that your horse, Mister Castle?'

'No ma'am. It's a Quarter Circle R horse. My horse is out back in the corral.'

She walked toward the rear of the barn without speaking or looking at Castle. He tagged after her, leaned on the topmost stringer as she was doing – and had a bad notion which she confirmed when she asked which was his horse. He pointed to a bay horse, a large animal with little pig eyes and a roman nose.

She studied the big bay horse, which had been shod recently. She stepped back looking at Castle. He knew why she had asked which his horse was, and shouldn't have been surprised when she said, 'That's not the horse you rode into our yard on, Mister Castle. Your bay horse wasn't roman-nosed, he wasn't that ugly.'

While Al and the handsome woman gazed at each other he thought of something an old man had told him one time: There were some things a man didn't need in this life, biting dogs, kicking mules and smart female-women.

He faced around toward the corral. 'No, not that big bay, the one behind him.'

The woman stepped ahead to lean on the stringer again. Something, a kindly fate maybe, had allowed Al's bay to stand in mud at the stone trough. His four feet were covered with mud to the hocks.

He leaned beside the woman to ask a question. 'Why are you interested in my horse?' He knew the answer but wanted her to put it into words.

She turned to face him. She had even features, a generous mouth and eyes the colour of steel dust. 'I think you know, Mister Castle. What don't make sense to me is that you'd stay in the country.'

She passed back up through the barn and halted in the front opening. Al was back beside the tied horse. She said, 'Did you see that man who was at the main-house last night?' And gave Castle no opportunity to reply. 'His name is Deacon Tuttle. He comes through every year or two buying cattle as he goes. He makes up a pretty good-sized herd. Sometimes it's too big for him to make a tally until he stops somewhere to let the critters graze while he takes stock ... Some time back Mister Black sold him some cattle, and delivered them along with a bill of sale. The reason he came back last night was that all those Quarter Circle R cattle was there when he road-branded them, and two days later some weren't there.'

Castle did not have to improvise on the spur of the moment this time, he knew what she was hinting before she finished. His reply was given in a believable manner. 'Miss Humphrey, as far back as you're talkin' about, and longer, I was on the far side of those big mountains.'

She answered sharply. 'But your horse wasn't. I was raised with horses. I pay attention to them anywhere I see them. More than I do to the riders ... Mister Castle, my paw and brothers got two dead men in our barn. They were our hired riders.'

Al sighed. 'Do me a favour, ma'm. Come right out an' say what you're beatin' around the bush about.'

She stood a long time gazing at him without speaking, but eventually she spoke, quieter this time, more direct. 'The poster, Mister Castle ... There was a Wanted dodger lying in the grass where our riders had been killed ... Last night I got to wondering why a man like you wouldn't have the sense at least to use another name.'

Al reddened. That damned dodger. He hadn't thought to look for it after the shooting.

Nan Humphrey left the barn walking toward the main-house. Al leaned on the horse he had intended to saddle for several minutes before moving. He was alone on the place with the woman and old Elijah. He had done those killings in self-defence. He had known those rustlers wouldn't allow him to reach the gate.

He had two choices, tell the truth and probably get hung for being the partner of the men who had really stolen the cattle. Or go tell old Elijah the truth – and that had precious little chance of working as long as the handsome woman was with the old man.

It occurred to him now, that his arriving at Corral Canyon the evening before, and being there when those two bearded thieves had driven the cattle in, would seem as though he had been an accomplice – otherwise how could he explain why he had been in there – a secret place? That he and his tired horse had followed wapiti and deer sign to the spring wouldn't sound very believable, not to an irate trail-driver, not to most cattlemen, and certainly not to anyone who had lost livestock to rustlers.

He led the tied horse out, turned him into the corral, caught his own animal and led it back inside to be saddled and bridled.

He worked fast, led the horse out the rear barn opening, mounted and rode steadily west until he was satisfied no one from the main-house could have seen him leave, then altered to a southerly course until sunset, then swung easterly. The country in that direction had looked empty, and right now and probably for the next few days he thought that was what he needed.

He made a dry camp after nightfall, was hobbling his animal when he noticed something that made his breath stop for three seconds. The bay horse had cast both front shoes.

There were places with soft, moist earth where that would not have mattered very much. The territory he was riding into was stony, grassy, in some areas there were abrasive granite chips as close as finger-width apart.

He did not rest well and was back in the saddle before dawn. He rode about a half mile before his horse threw up its head, little ears pointing. It was still too dark to see very far but Castle drew rein, sniffed a moment or two then swung to the ground to lead the horse. A mounted man even in pre-dawn light, showed up like a sore thumb.

He heard a band of antelope running ahead of his scent and paused to listen. It was a pleasant sound, much preferable to pursuing horsemen.

He tried to utilise soft earth when he could but there wasn't enough. Once a horse has been shod a few times his hooves softened. If he is never shod his hooves are hard as iron. To make matters worse for Al Castle, both his bay horse's front feet were white, the kind of hoof that wears down fast.

He stopped to make a smoke for breakfast and stand a long time looking back. The dawn was clear, visibility was excellent; there were no horsemen behind him.

Normally, Al was not much of a swearing man,

but this time, standing beside the horse trickling smoke he said, 'Son of a bitch!'

Fate was never predictable and rarely friendly. While leading the horse to favour it as much as possible in case he might need its strength later, was slow going, and the buildings he had been gratified not to have seen before, he now wished to see. Ideally, it might be an isolated ranch with a forge, an anvil, and some blank horseshoes.

He had made good time last night, and while his progress was much slower this morning, at least he saw no sign of pursuit and he looked back often.

Once, when he stopped at a piddling creek for the horse to drink, he told the totally disinterested animal that whoever managed the affairs of two-legged things had really worked a foolproof trap for Castle to ride into – with no inkling at all.

He left the piddling creek, went about a hundred feet and saw fresh shod-horse tracks paralleling him, veering in now and then before veering away. It could be innocent enough; some rangeman hunting strays or some pot-hunter after game to peddle in a town.

The land had very little cover, extremely few trees and only a few arroyos worthy of the name, and then considerable distance apart. He lost the tracks as he plodded in what he considered was a fairly straight line toward a horizon showing no rooftops and no livestock.

There should have been cattle, at least wild burros; the land was pretty well leached out but there was grass, pale rather than healthy green, but grass nevertheless.

With nothing else to think about he puzzled over the absence of grazing animals right up to the moment when he was trudging past several large, ancient grey stones and someone cocked a pistol.

5
Fate's Unfriendly Hand

Castle's initial reaction was astonishment. That lasted scant moments. Those tracks he had seen … What made his eyes wide was the voice from somewhere among the large stones.

'Get rid of the six-gun, Mister Castle.'

Her! How in the hell had she got …!

'*Drop it!*'

He lifted out the weapon and let it fall. She emerged cautiously with a cocked Colt in her fist. He could not believe she had out-ridden him, but clearly she had. He ignored the pistol. 'How in hell did you do it?' he asked.

The muscular, handsome woman – not pretty, not even particularly attractive, but handsome – was slow to reply, but she did.

'I guess you could say it was the difference between a horseman and a cattleman. Remember that big roman-nosed bay horse? He had more bottom and muscle than any two horses … I knew you'd run. When you were riding west I watched from the porch. I let you get a fair start. I saddled the ugly bay and lost you when you turned south,

but fresh tracks were easy to follow. I had to hang
far back until dark. I simply out-rode you – after I
found two worn out horseshoes.' She studied him
for a moment before also saying, 'There's
something I'd like to know. Why did you shoot
those men in Corral Canyon?'

He sighed, let all his weight rest on one side and
looked steadily at her. She was a woman a man
could tie to. He began at the beginning, told her
the truth and saw in her face she didn't believe
him. When he was finished she was still and
silent. Somewhere behind her among the big
rocks a thirsty horse pawed.

He said, 'Put up the gun, you don't need it.'

She made no move to holster the weapon; she
said, 'A horse thief is likely to be treacherous.
Would you like to know how my paw and brothers
figured it? Our two hired men had a couple of
friends that was new to the country. Paw didn't
trust them. They did their chores but was sort of
secretive. When they didn't come back paw and
my brothers went looking for them ... That canyon
where you'n the others drove those stolen Quarter
Circle R cattle was where my brothers go hunting
every autumn. They heard bawling cattle and
found them in the canyon – with the dead riders
and that Wanted dodger about you.'

Castle moved slightly to lean on his horse. 'I
told you the gospel truth. I found the canyon by
following game trails. I was asleep in the
sunshine when those two fellers with whiskers
showed up. They told me to ride out an' close the
gate ... Lady, I didn't come down in the last rain.
As I rode I reloaded my six-gun. When it was

ready I turned. One of those fellers had his six-gun up ready to shoot me. I shot first. That's the truth ... I never saw them before in my life until they awakened me at the spring.'

'But you tucked tail and ran after we talked at the barn,' she said.

'Yeah; what would you have done, a stranger in new country with a good chance if I didn't run someone'd hang me for a rustler.'

'And a killer, Mister Castle.'

They stood regarding each other through a long moment of silence. Something caught Castle's attention from the corner of his eye, a large, fat Gila monster who evidently lived among the rocks had climbed atop one to sun himself. He was less than six inches from the woman's gun-arm where it bent at the elbow.

He spoke very softly to her. 'Stand still. There's a Gila lizard on the rock beside your arm.'

Nan Humphrey did not take her eyes off Castle, her expression was sardonic. 'You could do better'n that.'

'Turn your head real slow – *real slow*.'

It may have been the sound of his voice, it may have been that she believed him, but in either case she obeyed, moving her head so slow it seemed hardly to be moving. She saw the ugly orange and black creature.

Castle spoke again, softly. 'Don't move. Keep your head turned.' He knelt very slowly, picked up his six-gun and fired from a crouch. Blood and entrails splattered the woman's face and shirt. She sprang sideways, raised a cuff to wipe her face.

Castle was standing erect, six-gun hanging at his side. In the same quiet voice he said, 'You owe me one, ma'm. Maybe you'd live through a rattler bite but never if one of those poisonous bastards bit you.'

He holstered his Colt and waited. She had nothing to say until she had shed as much of the Gila monster's parts from her blouse as she could and had again wiped her face.

She looked at Castle, still speechless, eased down the hammer of her weapon and sagged enough to have to use her left hand for support on the rock.

He smiled a little. 'Do you know this country?'

She shook her head.

'We need water, ma'm.'

Finally, she found her voice. 'Suppose you'd have missed?'

'I don't miss, not that close anyway. When I worked ranges in the north country with nothin' much to do, I spent my wages for bullets an' practised for weeks ... What do we do about water?'

She eased down on one of the rocks, recovering but still shaken. 'I didn't see it,' she said in an unsteady voice.

'You were facing me, it come up on your blind side ... Lady. Water!'

She inhaled deeply and exhaled. 'Water ... Go back where there is some.'

The roman-nosed horse was pawing again as though siding with Al Castle about the need for water. Nan Humphrey arose, glanced once at the gory rock where the Gila monster had been and looked away.

She was recovering faster now. 'I don't know this easterly country. I know my own country. I know where there is water back there.' She paused to run a slow gaze far out and around before also saying, 'I don't know ... It could be a mile and it could be a hundred miles.' She brought her attention back to Castle. 'If you want to go searching for it, go ahead. I'm going back.'

Castle went closer to the rocks and perched on one of them. He gazed at her a long time without speaking. It made her uncomfortable so she broke the silence. 'Leave. I'm not going to stop you. I'll go back and tell them I lost your tracks.'

Castle finally spoke. 'Lady, I wasn't part of those rustlers. What I told you is the truth. My horse an' I was tired. We followed that game trail ...'

'You've already told me that story, twice, Mister Castle.'

'And you don't believe it?'

' ... I don't know, but you kept me from getting poisoned. Like you said, I owe you – so get on your horse and keep going.'

He made a rueful smile at her. 'You found the wore out horseshoes. How far do you think a man could go in this country on a barefoot horse? At the most, five, six miles before he'd get too sore-footed to keep going.'

Her gunmetal eyes slowly widened on him. 'The roman nosed horse?'

'That'd leave you afoot out here. It's one hell of a long walk – and no water. Ma'm, we got us a big problem.'

She considered him for a moment then shifted

her gaze to his dozing horse, down to the pair of white hooves and back to Castle. 'Do you want to take a chance and trust me?' she asked. 'If you do I can go back, get water and return. Do you have any grub?'

'No.'

'I have. In my saddlebags. I'll leave it. I should be able to get back maybe tomorrow, late.' She stood up off the rock. He raised a hand. 'Your kin got that Wanted dodger?'

'Yes.'

He dropped the restraining hand and slowly wagged his head. Before he could speak she said, 'You don't trust me.'

For a fact Al Castle had reason not to trust people, even ones he had saved from dying of Gila monster venom.

She sank back down on the rock. 'Then I'll stay. You can ride my horse and I'll lead yours until we find water.'

He fell into another long silence. Right now, despite what his eyes told him, that this female-woman was muscled up like a man and had cracked someone's jaw, she didn't seem tough or treacherous. In fact the longer he sat there watching her, the more he liked what he saw.

Well hell; he wasn't going much farther unless he took her horse, which he did not intend to do, so that left him with a decision to make about taking her along with him, and something in the back of his head said that if he did that, and if her kinsmen found them, they'd shoot him sure as hell was hot for not only being a cattle thief but also a stealer of women.

She interrupted his thoughts again. 'I give you my word I'll come back with water.'

'Alone?'

Her expression changed; *that* was what had kept him silent so long. 'Yes, alone.'

He stood up. 'You're a good lookin' woman. Good lookin' women are just naturally treacherous.'

She flared at him. 'I'm *not* good looking. No one in my family thinks I'm good looking, and I'm not treacherous.' Her temper softened. 'But if I was, what choice do you have? And the longer we set here the hotter it'll get and the longer it'll take me to get back.'

He shifted his shell belt and replied without looking at her. 'I'll start back leadin' my horse.'

Without another word she worked her way to the rear of the boulder pile and returned astride the roman-nosed Quarter Circle R horse. She stopped beside him as though to speak. He spoke first. 'Who's lookin' after Mister Black?'

She shook her head. 'I don't know. Maybe his riders.'

He looked up at her until she blushed and shortened the reins. 'Do you like to argue, ma'm?' She shook her head. 'Well *I* say you are good lookin'.'

She almost spoke, was still blushing when she gigged the horse and started back the way she had come.

Castle watched her until she was small in the distance, then loosened the cinch on his bay horse, turned it back the way they had come and started walking.

It got hot as the day wore along. Both he and

the horse could have spit cotton if they could have
spit. By late afternoon when they came upon one
of those scraggly trees where there was shade,
they paused. The shade was minimal but they
needed rest, at least the critter with two legs
instead of four needed rest.

He rolled and lighted a smoke and while gazing
back the way they had come told the horse she
was good looking. Not like town womenfolk, but
she could match them if she had a chance to.

He remembered what Morris and Avery had
said and half-smiled in resignation. Maybe they
were right. Maybe they weren't, too. For a fact his
last half hour among those rocks with her she
hadn't seemed difficult.

He killed the smoke, led the horse along until
dusk before resting again. It was still hot and
would remain so until maybe midnight or a little
later.

He got a blister on one heel which caused him to
sit on the ground, remove his boot, tear a piece of
cloth off a shirt tail and make a bandage which he
knew would hurt more when he removed the
adhering piece of cloth without water, put the boot
back on and resumed walking. The blister let him
know it was still down there, but was less painful
than it had been.

Along toward dawn with a chill in the night he
told the horse he thought they'd maybe walked
eight or ten miles and if the horse didn't mind he
was going to lie down and sleep for a while. Just in
case the horse hadn't been listening he hobbled it,
removed the bridle so it could graze if it cared to,
pitched little rocks away and eased down on the

ground. To ameliorate the pain from his heel he removed one boot.

Some nights back at the Quarter Circle R he hadn't slept worth a damn. This particular night he was asleep almost before he'd closed his eyes.

The cold awakened him as the first streaks of dawn faintly brightened the eastern curve of the world. He could have slept on but didn't. He got up, swung his arms until circulation offset the chill, then looked for the horse. It wasn't in sight, but the dying night limited visibility. He sat down to up-end the boot from long habit, and a scorpion fell out, stood straight on its legs and moved its venomous tail and stinger from side to side. Castle scuffed sandy soil in its face until the creature hastened away.

He arose, gimped when the sore heel caused pain, and went in search of the horse. It wasn't far away, no more than a quarter mile where it had found tufts of buffalo grass. He led it back, put the bridle on and was tempted to ride, so he mounted and urged the horse along. It went well until it got a stone bruise and afterwards limped so badly he got down and led it.

If he lived to be a hundred he would never again pass a town with a smithy and not have new shoes put on all around.

The cold got no worse but neither did it get any better. He had to limp a little to favour the blistered heel; even walking on his toe made the boot rub the blister so he sat down, removed the boot, got up and started out barefoot on the sore foot.

That wasn't a great success either. He hadn't

gone barefoot since childhood and like a tender-footed horse, every tiny pebble felt like a full-blown rock.

Eventually the sun arose but for an hour afterward there was no appreciable heat in the new day. Castle halted scanning the onward country which was as empty of moving objects as it had been the day before.

He sought a shady place. There had been no trees since yesterday. There were no longer any boulders large enough for a man to hunker behind, but he made himself as small as he could on the lee side of a thornpin thicket, not close but close enough to rest.

He hadn't eaten, which bothered him equally with his thirst. If she came back with her brothers or cattlemen, he had bullets, a gun, and couldn't ride nor even walk very well. All anyone would have to do to take him would be sit out beyond six-gun range like a buzzard and wait.

His mind turned gloomy. She wouldn't fetch back water, she would fetch back armed men seeking a rustler who had killed his accomplices. She would stay back on her horse watching the men she had brought close in and shoot him.

6
A Long Ride Back

His horse whinnied. It was standing head up, ears forward, watching something Castle could not see until he arose behind the thornpin.

She was riding a different horse, a steady-going sorrel with big feet and muscle. She waved. Castle waved back – and squinted behind her as far as he could see, saw nothing, no movement, no rider-shapes and sank down as she came close, swung off and handed him one of several canteens she had looped around the saddle horn. As he raised it she watched, then stepped up and knocked the canteen aside. She did not say a word. Castle could have killed her. He raised the canteen again and this time she spoke from over beside Castle's horse. 'You want to get foundered? *Put it down!*'

Castle lowered the canteen, watched her tip another canteen so his horse could drink, and felt sweat bursting out under his skin.

She came back, sank to her knees and handed him a small packet wrapped in red checkered cloth, the kind folks used to cover dining tables with.

She watched him wolf down the food and shook her head thinking it was amazing how one day could change a man so much. Yesterday he had been a whole man, today he had an ugly blister on the foot with no boot or sock on it, his eyes were sunken, his movements were sluggish and his gaze seemed staring and dry.

She settled opposite him, waited until he had eaten and taken on as much water as he dared, then fished something from a shirt pocket and offered it to him. It was an unopened sack of tobacco with wheat straw papers. As he took it and thanked her she spoke gently to him. 'We can go back. My brothers went up to get those rustled Quarter Circle R cattle for the trail-driver who bought them, an' meet him north of Campton where he'll drive them to join his other critters ... Mister Black ...' She hesitated. 'I didn't tell my paw or brothers about you but I had to say something to Mister Black, so I told him your story.'

'An' he didn't believe it,' Castle said matter-of-factly.

She gave a little noncommittal shrug. 'I can't say whether he believed it or not, but those older men like my paw and Mister Black put a lot of store in what folks do, an' he told me about you taking his part in a fight with some rider. He said for me to bring you back to Quarter Circle R. He'd make sure no one made trouble for you.'

Castle was quiet for as long as was required to make a quirley and light it, then, trickling smoke he looked at her. He was beginning to feel human again. 'You *are* good looking.'

She stirred as though to arise. He held up one hand. 'Wait.'

'We got to start back ... *Mister* Castle.' She walked toward the dozing animals. With her back to him she said, 'We'll have to ride double.'

His horse trailed after them, it liked having company, and there was no place else to go. Castle had put his boot on but the blistered heel had swollen enough to cause pain, so he removed the boot, tied it to one of the saddle thongs, then squirreled around to sit square up again.

She did not say a word and, while most people who rode double held their arms around the waist of the person in the saddle, Castle balanced without holding to anything, until the sorrel horse stumbled, then he gripped the back of the cantle.

Nan Humphrey rode a little stiffly for the first few miles, then relaxed. She had nothing to say until they were far along. Eventually she said, 'I have an idea Deacon Tuttle, the trail-driver, may have told Tom Waters about the stolen cattle. I've known Tom a long time ...'

'The lawman in Campton?'

'Yes ... That's what troubles me, Mister Castle. Not countin' my paw and brothers, if the story spreads about you killing our two riders and being in the Corral Canyon with stolen cattle there'll be cowmen who might be troublesome.'

He rode a half mile in silence, then said, 'You're goin' to be in trouble helpin' me – stoppin' me from gettin' out of the country.'

She had obviously thought about those things

too, because she replied in a voice that she forced
to be light. 'All I did was keep you from maybe
getting lost without water. And fetching you
back.' She reined around a torpid rattlesnake that
didn't even coil and rattle. He looked to Al to be
full of baby mice.

He waited until the rattler was behind then
said, 'I wish you'd believe me.'

'I'd like to, Mister Castle. Trouble is – I got
doubts about the others believing you … Maybe
what we ought to do is get you back to feeling
good, give you another horse and next time set
you to riding due south where there's creeks and
good grass.'

He dryly said, 'A fresh-shod horse, Miss
Humphrey?'

She chuckled. 'A fresh-shod horse, Mister
Castle.'

The sun had moved on its inexorable course.
Now, they had it in their faces. Castle pulled his
hatbrim so low he had to tilt his head to watch the
land ahead. Nan Humphrey did not have a hat.
He offered her his hat. She said, 'What will you do
without it?'

She held out her hand, he gave her the hat and
hunkered. It was awkward and made it difficult to
retain his balance. She said, 'Put your arms
around me.'

They rode that way for several miles when he
felt her stiffen. 'Riders,' she exclaimed.

He raised up, saw the pair of horsemen coming
toward them at a walk, said nothing until he
recognised them and told her it was the Quarter
Circle R men, Avery and Morris. She had to tilt

her head to verify the identification. She still did not relax. 'How did they know to come down here?' she asked.

'Old man Black most likely sent 'em.'

'Friends of yours?'

'Well; up to now they've been friends. I'd guess it depends on what they know – what the old man maybe told them.'

'He told me he wouldn't tell anyone.'

Evidently he hadn't because both riders raised their right arms in salute, and when they were closer Morris called to Castle. 'You tryin' to do what Dowd did; ride off without collecting your wages?' That didn't sound like old man Black had told them any more than to ride easterly.

Nan stopped, the Quarter Circle R riders came up, halted and sat gazing at Castle. Avery finally spoke. 'You look like a pigeon kicked you in the belly. What's wrong with your foot?'

'Got a blister,' Castle replied.

As the trio resumed their way Avery addressed the woman. 'Your paw come to the yard. Him an' the old man talked. I got no idea what it was about but your paw left the yard in a lope ridin' north.'

'Were my brothers with him?'

'No ma'm. He was alone.'

Morris added a little more. 'When he left the yard he looked grim as death.'

Morris and Avery rode in silence, occasionally looking at Al Castle, they were clearly curious and interested. Nan spoke to Castle without looking around. 'Tell them.'

Castle did; he started at the beginning and told

them the identical story he had told the woman. Avery looked shocked but Morris, a raffish man worked a cud of mule shoe into his cheek, expectorated once, then wagged his head in Castle's direction. 'I ain't real surprised. You asked a lot of questions about the Humphreys.' He expectorated again before also saying, 'I don't know what the marshal's goin' to say about all this.'

The silence returned as they plodded along. The sun sank lower, rested briefly atop a distant peak then began to gradually slide down its far side.

The heat remained but the sky began to lose some of its brassy appearance. Morris asked Nan Humphrey how she'd got the blood on her shirt. She told him, and another silence settled.

Avery broke it by asking a question. 'If them rustlers you nailed in the mountains had friends – who would they be?'

Castle shook his head. He had no idea, nor did it seem relevant until Avery also said, 'They got to be found – alive – Al, or you won't look real good.'

Castle smiled at Avery whose words implied belief in his story. It was good to have someone who didn't think he was a liar.

Later, with rooftops in sight, Nan spoke to Al Castle. 'I'll leave you in the yard. I want to go find my paw.'

Morris wagged his head, 'Nan, he won't believe it.'

'I think my youngest brother might. He and I are the closest. Anyway, it'll be all over the country and someone should be told *his* side.'

Avery and Morris rode along in solemn silence,

their faces hinted at their thoughts, which were simple enough: With no way to prove what he had said, Al Castle was a good candidate for a hang rope. If the stockmen got him before Marshal Waters knew Nan had brought him back, no one would ever see Al Castle again. The stockmen had taken care of things like this for many years. Rustlers, horse thieves and the like just simply disappeared. There was an awful lot of country where unmarked graves would keep secrets forever.

They entered the yard ahead of dusk. Nan took Castle to the main-house. Morris and Avery took care of the horses, of which only one, Castle's bay, had to be driven away from the trough three times, was not allowed to drink his full, was put into a corral and Morris forked timothy hay to him then leaned on a stringer until Avery came up. Morris said, 'Too bad his horse came up castin' its shoes. Avery, I wouldn't bet a plug of mule shoe on his chances.'

Avery watched the white-footed bay horse scarfing up hay like he hadn't eaten in a while, which he hadn't. 'What do you think, Morris?'

The shorter man wagged his head. 'It don't matter what I believe. The old man's goin' to get into this mess up to his hocks, an' I work for the old man ... As far as I know there's nothin' says I got to like the old son of a bitch, but I take his money, an' so do you.'

Before they got to the bunkhouse there was a light over in the main-house where a soiled, beard-stubbled Al Castle, carrying one boot, with blood-shot eyes and gaunt cheeks sank into a chair Nan pushed behind him.

The old man propped up in bed stared, then told Nan to fetch whiskey from the kitchen cupboard. Al didn't notice the old man's previously blurred speech had almost no blur in it.

While Nan was gone the old man squirmed around under his blankets until he was facing Castle, and said, 'Boy, I got to tell you, when you bought into my scrap with Dowd, I figured you was one of them fellers that trouble just sort of gravitated to, an' this time you're in it up to your gullet.'

Nan returned with the whiskey and two glasses. She tipped whiskey into both glasses and handed them to the men. Her face was expressionless. Elijah half drained his glass, mopped at watering eyes and put the glass aside.

The last slight slur left Elijah's words as he again addressed the bone-weary man on the chair holding one boot and marvelling at how fast the whiskey was working.

'I owe you, boy,' Elijah said. 'I always pay my debts. If they come out from town the next day or two to haul you back with 'em – you're not going.'

Nan interrupted to tell the old man she would go home. Elijah nodded, his immediate concern was the man on the chair at bedside. As she started away Al said, 'I mean it.' He didn't explain what he meant but as the woman passed his chair she rested a hand on his shoulder and squeezed.

The old man drained his glass and leaned slightly, red in the face with sparkling bright faded old eyes. 'You settle in at the bunkhouse. We'll talk again in the mornin'.'

Castle was feeling better than he'd felt in several days. He told Elijah all he needed was a strong horse – with good shoes on him – and this time he'd ride south.

The old man snorted. 'Boy, you listen to me; this story will be all over the countryside come tomorrow. You wouldn't get five miles, good horse or not. If they catch you runnin', you won't stand the chance of a snowball in hell. They'll hang you as sure as night follers day ... You stay here.' The old man glared. 'The only friends you got right now is in this yard ... Go down yonder, eat supper an' climb into a bunk. An' tomorrow you stay close. Morris an' Avery ... I'll talk to them. They been lookin' for drift. Not tomorrow. They'll stay close tomorrow. You care to refill your glass?'

As Al stood up lightheadedness struck. He shook his head at the old man. 'One more,' he said, 'an' I wouldn't be able to find my rear end with both hands.'

Elijah stared. 'I want your word. You won't try to sneak away in the night. I want your word you'll stay close.'

Al nodded and smiled. 'You got it. To tell you the bald truth, the way I feel right now I'd go to sleep standin' up in hell.'

At the bunkhouse Al smelled cooked food before he reached the porch. When he walked in the lighted lamp made him squint. Avery and Morris were already at the table. Morris gestured toward the stove and went on eating, but Avery said, 'You better soak off that rag on your heel, an' smear the blister with bear grease.'

Al flung the useless boot on the bunk he had

used, filled a plate at the stove, limped to the table and sat down without saying a word. Avery and Morris, respecters of the notion that if a man figured to talk, fine, if he figured to eat, that was fine too, but doing both at the same time was like watering a horse with the bit in its mouth, the eating man and the drinking horse sucked air, which was unpleasant.

Castle crawled into the bunk, turned on his side and was dead to the world in moments. Avery was drying the plates when he eyed the exhausted man and spoke to Morris, who was washing dishes.

'I guess he's good with a gun, but it won't help him with the kind of trouble he's in now – unless he can find a gun that'll shoot about fifteen times without re-loading.'

Morris had nothing to say as he went to the rear door, flung the water out, returned to hang the pan from its nail and roll his sleeves down as he too considered the man in the bunk. When he spoke it had little to do with Al Castle.

'Amos and Martin Humphrey's as likely to believe that story as I am to sprout wings. I'd give a pretty to know what the old man told him.'

Avery hazarded a knowledgeable guess. 'He told Al to stay close to the yard tomorrow. Likely, he'll tell us the same thing.' Morris sighed, sank down at the table and leaned. It had been another long day under an unfriendly sun. 'Nan ... I think she's taken a shine to Castle.'

'Well; he kept her from gettin' bit by a poisonous lizard.'

'Yeah. But I don't mean that. On the ride back

she acted like she didn't object to him holdin' her around the middle.'

Avery went to his bunk, sat down to kick out of his boots, shed his belt and holstered Colt, drape his hat from a nail and lie back wiggling his toes as he regarded Morris. 'Go to bed,' he said. 'Blow out the lamp an' go to bed.'

Morris did exactly as he'd been told, but he was still faintly frowning when he swung up both legs atop the bunk.

They both got a surprise come morning. There was smoke coming from the kitchen stovepipe at the main-house. There was no way Elijah had stoked up a fire. Out back they looked at the corralled horses. One had drying sweat on its neck. Morris said, 'It's the sorrel she rode yestiddy.'

Later, when Castle came out limping but wearing his boot, Nan came marching from the main-house, she ignored Castle, went to the barn and told the riders in there that Elijah did not want them to leave the yard today. She then turned on her heel, went to the bunkhouse porch, nodded to Castle and held out her hand. There was an ivory-handled straight razor on her palm. 'You'll look better,' she told him as he took the razor, and added a little more with her head slightly cocked, 'It wouldn't hurt if you bathed in the creek, either ... How do you feel?'

'Alive. Is that good enough?' He had bristled a little at her remark about him needing a bath.

She ignored his pique. 'My paw will ride over directly.'

'Did he believe you, Nan?'

'No. Paw and my oldest brother, Martin,

wouldn't. My youngest brother would. They're both
fetching those stolen cattle down out of that
canyon. Pete's always been my favourite.'

She left him on her way back to the main-house.
He watched her right up until she looked back as
she opened the door, and looked like she had
smiled, but he couldn't be sure, the next moment
the door closed behind her. Also, it was just barely
full daylight.

He limped down to the barn where Morris saw
the straight razor protruding from his shirt pocket,
and leaned on his three-tined fork. 'That's Elijah's
razor,' he said which brought Avery around to look.

'She told me to shave an' take an all-over bath.'

Both men laughed but said nothing more, not
until Al had gone back to the bunkhouse for a towel
and a chunk of brown lye soap, then Morris
repeated what he'd said before. 'She's sweet on
him.'

Avery looked unconvinced. 'Why? Because she
loaned him Elijah's razor? Hell, Elijah's not going
to be able to shave himself for a while if ever. An'
for a fact he smells like a tanyard. I noticed that
last night when I got up an' opened the door.'

The new-day warmth was slow arriving; one
reason was the build-up of cloud galleons coming
with incredible slowness from beyond some distant
northeasterly mountains. Rain would be welcome,
but it did no good to believe it would arrive; for
about half as many times as those huge white
clouds hung over the Campton countryside they
sailed tantalisingly away to dump water somewhere else. Maybe atop rocky mountains where all
the water did was run off.

Castle shaved; Elijah's razor was surprisingly sharp. He went to the creek, found a place where willows provided adequate protection from wandering females, bathed, sat on a rock until he was half dry, used the towel for his hair, dressed and limped back to the yard – and got a surprise. There was a saddle animal at the main-house tie-rack.

It required no particular sleuthing ability to guess who had ridden that animal, which had a neat left-shoulder brand; it was the spade used on playing cards. He had no idea what the Humphrey brand was but he could guess.

Avery and Morris were over at the shoeing shed shaping blanks at the forge and anvil, pitching them into a pile for later use.

It was hot in the shed although it only had three sides, was wide open in front.

Morris was drinking from an olla when Castle entered. Avery was working the forge. He was dripping sweat but as he turned the crank he saw Castle and released the handle, which continued to turn a few times.

He came over where Castle was standing and said 'Amos Humphrey's at the main-house. He's been in there quite a spell.'

Morris wiped his chin and took out a sweat-softened chewing plug. After getting it snugged into place and expectorating once, he eased down on the anvil and shook his head. 'I got a bad feeling,' he told the other two men. 'Maybe you should have rode on last night.'

Castle's reply to that was brusque. 'I promised the old man I wouldn't.'

'Well,' stated Morris, 'I think it would have been a good idea anyway. The old man's judgment ain't always a hunnerd percent right. As sure as we're sittin' here the damned sky's goin' to open up an' rain trouble on all of us.'

Castle said, 'I'll go over there.'

'What can you tell 'em? They already know your story. Amos is a hard-headed feller. Tougher'n a boiled owl. I'd stay clear if I was you.'

Avery was nodding agreement when someone called from the main-house porch. Nan was standing out there. Castle stepped into the sunshine. She gestured for him to come to the house. As he started across the yard Morris rolled his eyes heavenward and Avery went back to his forge, expressionless and slow to crank the forge handle again.

7
Show Down!

Castle did not know the large man waiting at bedside when Castle returned with the large, older man's daughter. He looked doggedly unrelenting as Nan introduced him, neither offered a hand nor a greeting.

Elijah, under his old quilts, jerked and wiggled like a squirrel. Nan spoke to her father ignoring the other two.

'I told you, paw. If I'd moved that Gila monster'd have bit me sure.'

Amos Humphrey switched his attention back to Al Castle, being a man who set great store by favours, particularly to the favour Castle had done by saving his daughter's life, he hung fire for a long time before speaking. 'I'm not sayin' you stumbled into Corral Canyon. Maybe you did an' maybe you didn't. What I'm sayin' is that I got a Wanted dodger on you, an' bein' an outlaw makes it hard for me to think you wasn't one of the rustlers.'

It was quite a speech. Elijah asked Nan to fetch the bottle from the kitchen, then addressed the

81

large, grey and craggy man. 'Like I told you, Amos, he took my part on the porch.'

Amos Humphrey gazed toward the bed. 'There's no accountin' for things folks do, Elijah. What counts now is that he's an outlaw, and those two hired riders of mine was most likely outlaws even before they went to work for me. For a fact I know they was rustlers – now. An' for a fact, this feller was in the canyon when he killed them.'

Nan was in the doorway holding the bottle. She spoke directly to her father. 'Why, paw?'

'I don't know. He can tell us maybe. They could've got into a fight over the cattle, maybe they never liked each other.'

Elijah snorted. 'Maybes ain't good enough, Amos. He done you a favour an' he sure-hell done me one. I'm no angel an' neither are you. That's good enough for me; it ought to be good enough for you.'

Amos Humphrey sought a chair, found one on the far side of the bed, sat down and looked from his daughter to Al Castle. 'There's somethin' else, Elijah. When he come into our yard after killin' my hired men, he sneaked in from the east. He done that to make us believe he hadn't come from the north. Now, why would he do that if he wasn't bein' clever?'

Castle interrupted the exchange between the older men. 'You're right, I made a sashay so's it'd look like I come from the east. Mister Humphrey, I was green as grass to this country. For all I knew you could have been a rustler too; the tracks of those riders came from your yard straight to the Corral Canyon. Like I said, I was walkin' on eggs. I didn't know anyone, never been in the country before ... What would you have done, ride right into that yard with three armed men on the porch, an' say I'd killed two rustlers and knew where the cattle were?'

Elijah smiled crookedly. For the rest of his life his smile would be crooked. Before he could speak Nan moved to bedside, handed Elijah the bottle, straightened up and looked directly at her father.

'Paw; why are you setting in judgment? They weren't your cattle. Except for being a neighbour of Elijah, it's none of our business.'

Her father flared up at her. 'It *is* our problem! It's the problem of every cow rancher in the country!'

Castle looked at the woman and shook his head. 'You're not goin' to change his mind, so leave it be.'

She faced around, eyes narrowed. 'Leave it be? They'll hang you!'

Elijah said, 'No they won't. Nobody's goin' to take a rider of mine off my land unless they want to fight for him, an' they might not do it even then.' Elijah faced the larger but equally as old man sitting on the off-side of his bed. 'Amos, like she said, it wasn't your cattle. It was mine. When your boys deliver 'em to that trail-driving free-grazer, that's the end of it as far as I'm concerned.'

Humphrey was not a yielding individual, and there was the matter of his two dead riders. 'All right, Elijah; I think rustling's every cowman's business, but leave that be. How about murder? Tell me that ain't everyone's business.'

Castle made a little hopeless gesture. He even

smiled slightly at Amos Humphrey. Nan interrupted before Castle could speak. 'Paw, you said it yourself – you didn't trust those men.'

Humphrey sounded more exasperated than angry when he replied to his daughter. 'Nan, they never got off a shot. For a fact I didn't cotton to them men, but....'

'Paw, I told you he shot that Gila monster. I didn't tell you how: His gun was on the ground. He bent, got it an' shot the lizard off the rock no more'n six inches from my arm.'

Amos gazed quizzically at his daughter.

'He shot those two rustlers the same way.'

'How do you know that, Nan?'

The woman also looked exasperated when she replied. 'Don't be so damned pig-headed, paw. That's the only way he could have shot them both, by bein' lightnin' fast. Faster than they were.'

Elijah nipped from the bottle, wiped the rim and offered it to Humphrey, who ignored it to stare from his daughter to Al Castle. He stood up. 'Unload your gun,' he told Castle, who obeyed without a word until they were facing one another, then he said, 'Unload yours.'

Humphrey shucked out all the loads. He sank the Colt into its holster, looked steadily at the younger man across the bed and barely inclined his head.

Nan and Elijah seemed not to be breathing. Castle's six-gun was being cocked on the rise. Amos Humphrey's gun was only half clear of leather.

Amos sank the gun and said, 'Again.'

The same thing happened. Amos let the six-gun

drop back into its holster as Elijah crowed. 'You satisfied? I seen him do that before when me'n a rider named Dowd got into it. Only that time the gun was loaded.'

Humphrey sat back down. His daughter said, 'Paw ...?'

The large old man nodded. 'Maybe.'

She exploded. 'Maybe! You're being stubborn. You've always been stubborn.' She flung around and left the room. Elijah held out the bottle again, this time toward Castle, who took it, tilted it once and leaned across the bed holding the bottle toward Nan's father. He considered the bottle, the extended arm and the face of the man holding it. Elijah was disgusted. 'You danged old screwt – *take it!*'

Humphrey took the bottle, swallowed twice and handed it to Elijah. He blew out a flammable breath before addressing Al Castle. 'One question: Was it just them two?'

'Yes.'

Humphrey dropped his head to study big work-roughened hands before speaking again. 'They had friends. I don't know, but one of my boys saw them talkin' real cozy at a poker table table in the Campton saloon. It wouldn't have meant much but they told me they'd never been in the country before and didn't know no one another.'

Humphrey raised his eyes to the younger man. 'I'm not comfortable about believin' you.'

Elijah's exasperation exploded exactly as Nan's had, only old Elijah's face was red and his eyes were watering. 'Amos, we been neighbours a long time. We been friends, most of that time. I always knew you was pig-headed, opinionated an' cranky at times. I never knew until this moment that you was also a damned fool! The lad didn't have a hand in stealin' those cattle! He didn't lie about what happened up there! If you wasn't such a....'

Nan appeared in the doorway. 'Riders coming.'

Elijah's mouth was still open but his mind had changed instantly. 'How far?'

'Mile, maybe a tad more.'

'How many?'

Nan answered as quietly as she'd spoken when she first announced the oncoming horsemen. 'Six ... They're too far, but the sun's shining off butt plates. They got booted saddleguns.' She let that fall into the silence for a moment before also saying, 'I can't be sure at that distance, but the man in the lead could be Marshal Waters.'

For ten seconds there was absolute silence in the room, then Elijah said, 'Fetch Morris an' Avery, Nan – please.'

She left the room, moments later the men heard the door slam out front. Humphrey broke the silence. 'I wish Martin an' Pete was here.'

Neither Elijah or Al commented about that. Al left the room to go out to the porch. If it was the marshal with posse-riders, they were taking their time. He was joined on the porch by Nan, Morris and Avery.

They stood watching the oncoming riders, silent until Nan spoke. 'Well; it's up to you, Mister Castle.'

Without turning Castle said, 'Al, just plain Al.'

She did not reply. Avery stepped back and sank into a chair. 'Bad odds,' he said quietly, also watching the riders.

Morris replied curtly. 'Not too bad, us three, the old man makes four.'

Avery regarded Morris from the chair. 'The old man's down in bed. It's you'n me an' Al.'

Nan looked at Avery without speaking.

Her father emerged from the house, squinted out where the horsemen were approaching, and blew out a ragged big sigh. ' ... Mister Castle?'

Al turned. 'I'll go with them.'

Nan stiffened. 'No you won't. Paw, can you see who three of those men are?'

Humphrey nodded without looking at his daughter. 'Forrest, Morgan, Len Cunningham an' Eustis Blount.'

His daughter said, 'Cattlemen.'

Humphrey went back inside. He wasn't gone long and when he returned he was holding a double-barrelled shotgun. Morris looked from the weapon to Humphrey's face, and smiled. Now there were four of them on the porch, the odds had been whittled a little.

Elijah was hollering from inside. Nan went to his bedroom. Elijah had got out of bed, had got one leg into his trousers, had lost his balance and had fallen. She stood in the doorway watching him groping and falling. He was swearing a blue streak. She came up behind the old man, picked him up and put him back on the bed. He was sputtering. It was humiliating enough being manhandled by a female-woman, it was even worse that she stood over him with his shellbelt and holstered Colt looped over one shoulder.

She levelled a rigid finger. 'You don't leave that

bed. No matter what, you don't try that again.'

Elijah's agitation made him drool. Nan snatched a towel from a chair-back, pushed Elijah flat down with one hand and roughly wiped his mouth with the other hand. Their faces were less than a foot apart. The old man swung his head away from the towel and glared. 'I know what you're doin',' he said in a slurred tone of voice. 'You're tryin' to save Al Castle's bacon. I seen how you looked at him.'

She leaned with the balled towel held tightly against his mouth. He made noises behind it, their faces were close, his red and agitated, hers calm and determined. She smiled at the old man.

'I owe him, Mister Black.'

She started to straighten up and slacken her hold on the towel. He said, 'You owe him? You don't owe him, you brought him back to safety. That wipes out you owin' him. Nan ... I'm old. I was married a long time, an' before that I did my share of courtin'. I know the way you was lookin' at him.'

She moved to stifle him again with the towel. He threw up an arm as he said a little more. 'You hid it from your paw an' the others ... I'm glad for you, girl. You deserve better'n havin' to cook for your paw and brothers ... I think he's a good man. He don't have much but between the two of you....'

She clamped down with the towel. Elijah had said about all he'd intended to say but held up a hand indicating he wasn't quite finished. She eased the towel up a few inches.

He spoke in a rambling voice, slurring his words again. 'Let me be best man at the weddin' and I'll make a decent wedding present of a couple thousand acres and a couple hunnerd head of cattle to start out with.'

She took the towel away and stood looking down, almost expressionless but not quite as she said, 'My paw should be best man.'

Elijah scoffed. 'He can be second best man.'

Outside men were calling greetings to one another. Nan pointed a stiff finger. 'If you get out of that bed one more time I'll come back, take your drawers off an' carry you outside.'

Elijah's imagination made him red as a beet long after she had left with his shellbelt and holstered Colt slung over a shoulder.

He got as near the upper bedposts as he could straining to hear but except for the called greetings and a few loud words he could not distinguish much. He picked up the bottle.

The town marshal entered the yard looking solemn as a judge. He and the posse riders he'd brought along were silent as they approached the front of the house. Avery beat the lawman to the act of initiating speech. He said, 'You gents look like you're goin' bear hunting.'

Marshal Waters and the men around him were not in the mood for levity. Waters leaned with both hands on the saddlehorn gazing from Amos Humphrey holding the scattergun, to Morris and Avery whose tie-downs were hanging loose, to Al Castle. His gaze remained there longest.

He said, 'How's Elijah?'

For a moment no one spoke, then Nan said, 'Better'n he's got a right to expect. He's in the house if you want to see him.'

The marshal's gaze drifted back to Al Castle. He didn't raise his voice as he said, 'I got a warrant for your arrest.' He added nothing to that such as shed your sidearm. They faced each other like stone images.

Morris frowned. 'For what?'

'Rustlin' an' murder.'

Morris rolled his eyes. 'When did he do them things?'

'Awhile back. He'd know.'

Morris was going to speak again when Nan spoke first. 'Give us a date ... Because whatever day you say I'll tell you straight out he was with me on that day.'

Tom Waters eyed the muscular woman soberly. 'Nan, don't get mixed up in this.'

Her father spoke holding the levelled shotgun. 'We're all mixed up in it, Tom. Mister Castle was with my daughter like she said. I'll take an oath to it.'

'Do you know what day, Amos?'

'She already told you. Whatever day you say he did something you don't like.'

One of the possemen was Jeb Devlin, Campton's saloonman. He made a scarcely audible snickering sound. When the men on both sides looked disapprovingly, the saloonman seemed not to notice.

A cowman behind the marshal addressed his fellow-cowman. 'It's rustlin' Amos. Rustlin' an' murder – in cold blood.'

Castle spoke. 'Who did I murder?'

Waters loosened in the saddle as he replied. 'Two rangemen. I was told they worked for Mister Humphrey.'

'How did I murder 'em, Marshal?'

'Shot 'em both. I got their hand guns in town. They never got off a shot.'

'Was you there when I shot them, Marshal?'

Tom Waters shook his head.

'Then how do you know I shot them, an' why did you say I rustled cattle?'

'I got two witnesses back in town. For safe keepin' I locked them in the jailhouse.'

Avery, silent up until now, got out of his chair, leaned on the railing between Morris and Castle, and addressed the lawman. 'You figure to take Al to jail?'

'Yes. An' I'm goin' to do it.'

To the left of the men at the railing Amos Humphrey pulled back both hammers of his scattergun. That got everyone's attention, but mostly among the men sitting on horses with no cover a couple of yards in front. One man eased his right hand down to ease the tie-down loose over his holster. Humphrey said, 'Put both hands on the saddle horn. All of you. If you're feelin' real brave, don't do it. Go for your weapons.' He lowered the shotgun slightly so that it was chest high to the posse riders.

Marshal Waters knew the townsmen with him. They wouldn't do anything as ridiculous as drawing against that cocked and aimed shotgun, but although he was acquainted with the stockmen, he was not at all sure they wouldn't precipitate a fight – and the marshal was out front. If Amos Humphrey fired both those barrels there wouldn't be enough of him and the closest posseman to carry back in a coffee can.

The saloonman broke the tense silence by addressing Al Castle. 'Go back with us, mister. I got friends; we'll make sure no one gets up a lynching party. If you don't, you're likely to be responsible for what'll happen in this yard, an' personally I wouldn't want anythin' like that on my conscience.'

Silence settled again. Humphrey's shotgun did not waver. The men in front of it could see his finger curled inside the triggerguard. One trigger was behind the other.

Nan said, 'I'll ride back with Mister Castle. You can lock me up too.'

Avery and Morris straightened up off the porch railing. Morris said, 'We'll go back with you too.' Avery nodded agreement.

Only big Amos Humphrey did not speak. He was watching the marshal and his riders. He did not look like he would hesitate to yank those two triggers.

Again Jeb Devlin the saloonman spoke. 'Let's get on our way, Marshal. They'll have likely kicked in the saloon's doors by now.'

A grizzled, shrewd-eyed cowman named Cunningham spoke quietly to the lawman. 'It's the best you're goin' to get Tom. Take it. At least we got the son of a bitch.'

8
Questions Without Answers

On the ride to town no one thought of helpless Elijah until Morris remembered and looked at Nan. She interpreted the look correctly. 'He can get to water. There's grub in the cooler. Exercise is good for a man in his condition.'

No one disputed her; for the time being Elijah Black was not worth thinking about. It was the town ahead and its inhabitants that increasingly worried Avery, who by nature was less bellicose than wary.

Cattle thieves ranked a very close second to horse thieves. Marshal Waters dropped back to ride between Castle and Nan Humphrey. He looped the reins, rolled and lighted a smoke, looked at Castle and said, 'You made some worthwhile friends for someone who's new to the country.'

Castle neither looked at the marshal nor spoke. Up ahead were the rooftops, water towers and wisps of stove smoke of Campton.

Waters turned to Nan, inhaled, exhaled,

decided from her profile this was not a good time and eased up to the lead again.

Inevitably when the town marshal had recruited his posse, of which townsmen were part, the reason for this spread throughout Campton. When the posse-riders returned with five people more than they had left with, one of them a woman, another her father, two Quarter Circle R riders and another individual most of them did not know, it was reasonable for word to be passed so that when the cavalcade passed through town as far as the jailhouse, there were onlookers on both sides of the road.

Marshal Waters left the caring of the animals to several possemen before herding his hostages into the jailhouse and barring the door from the inside as he told Morris, Avery and Castle to put their sidearms on his desk. As they moved to obey the marshal gazed dispassionately at Amos Humphrey, crossed to Amos's bench and held out his hand. The large older man handed over his sidearm and the scattergun. He and the lawman were wooden-faced.

Waters returned to his desk, perched on the edge of it, eyed his hostages as he rolled and lighted a smoke, then addressed Nan's father. He neither raised his voice nor sounded particularly antagonistic.

'I ought to tell you, Amos, there was some talk of you bein' involved with those rustlers. Two of 'em worked for you.'

Humphrey snorted. 'Do I look that stupid, Tom? Stealin' branded cattle from a neighbour; I don't need more cattle an' sure-Lord have never had truck with rustlers. Anybody who knows me would know that ... What you got is some flannelmouths here in town that don't have the sense gawd give a chicken. If you listen to folks like that, I'll be real disappointed in you.'

Normally, Amos Humphrey was not given to long statements, but this was not a normal situation.

Waters nodded and shifted his attention to Al Castle. If he'd had that Wanted dodger his attitude certainly would have been different, but the poster was on a table at the Humphrey place.

He said, 'Mister Castle, I got two men in my cells that I want to show you.' Waters paused before adding more. 'One's named Bishop, the other man calls himself Morrison. Those names mean anything to you?'

Al shook his head. As nearly as he could recollect he had never heard of Bishop or Morrison. He asked why they were in jail.

Water's reply was quietly given in a voice that was straightforward. 'They were up-country when Mister Humphrey's boys was driving cattle down to the road. They got belligerent, accused Martin and Pete Humphrey of stealin' cattle. Martin's not the kind of man to take kindly to that kind of talk. While Morrison and Bishop were arguin' with Pete, Martin used his six-gun to stop the argument. Martin an' Pete tied their arms behind their backs, removed their bridles an' led 'em along until they got the cattle north of town where a feller named Deacon Tuttle an' a Messican took 'em over. Martin an' Pete brought Bishop and Morrison to me at the jailhouse. They cussed me out good when I refused to untie 'em, so I locked 'em in a cell.'

Amos said, 'One time in town my boys saw those two rustlers who worked for me talkin' at the saloon with two strangers. If Martin an' Pete are still around town....'

Water shook his head as he interrupted. 'Your boys left for home. By now they'd ought to be out there.'

'Well, send for 'em,' Humphrey exclaimed.

The lawman went around to sit at his desk as he said, 'Why?'

Amos looked exasperated even before speaking. 'Why? Because if they got upset over Martin an' Pete drivin' them cattle down from Corral Canyon ... Ain't it clear to you, Tom?'

'No.'

'Who would even know there was cattle in the mountains? Why would they get all upset seein' those critters being driven down from there?'

The marshal leaned on his desk. 'They knew the pair that Castle killed?'

This time the cowman let his temper out a notch. 'You want me to paint it on the wall for you?'

Waters almost smiled at the irate stockman. 'No ... I just want 'em to see Mister Castle is all.' Waters arose. 'You folks stand up. See that reinforced door with all the bolts in it? Well, that leads to the cells down a narrow hallway. Amos, I want you to be first. The others walk behind you single file. Mister Castle, you stay back with me.' The lawman took a ring of keys from a peg in the wall and nodded for the large older man to open the door and start walking. As Humphrey moved to do this, Marshal Waters took Al Castle by the arm to hold him back until the others, including Nan Humphrey, followed Amos in single file.

There was not a sound until Nan passed a cell with two confined men standing against the front steel straps of their cage looking out. One of the men cat-called and said there was plenty of room in his cell if Nan got crowded where that lawman would put her.

She did not so much as turn her head, which seemed to encourage the cat-caller. He added more by saying, 'You're my kind of lady, ma'm, big enough for a man to wrestle to the ground.'

He was going to say more. Nan stopped, turned, went back to the men standing behind straps of steel, looked the man who had spoken in the eye – and swung.

His cell-companion squawked and jumped backwards as far as he could. The other man went over backwards wind-milling with both arms to break his fall. There was a flung-back streamer of blood from a torn lip. He was dazed, remained on the floor until Tom Waters and Al Castle appeared in front of the cell, then he and his companion only indifferently looked at Castle before beginning a loud and profane denunciation of the lawman.

Waters locked the others in, took Castle back to the office and bolted the cell-room door from his office-side, gestured for Al to sit on the bench opposite the desk, re-hung the keys on a wall peg, turned and said, 'That was Morrison an' Bishop. Do you know them?'

'Never saw either of 'em as far as I know … I'd guess neither of them knew Nan, either.'

Waters ruefully smiled. 'I guess not … Well, Mister Castle, they didn't seem to know you. They could be good actors, but it don't seem likely.'

Castle got comfortable on the bench gazing over at the marshal. 'I told you – I never saw those men before; never saw the men in the canyon before either.'

'I'd guess those two knew the fellers in the canyon. My guess is that it was one hell of a surprise when they come on to the Humphrey boys drivin' those cattle … Right now, Mister Castle, I'm about half convinced you had nothin' to do with those stolen cattle.'

Al sighed. If Nan's father didn't tell the marshal about that Wanted dodger … He said, 'How long are you goin' to hold me?'

Waters tipped back in his chair. 'At least until I've had a chance to question Bishop and Morrison.'

Castle's gaze widened. 'You haven't done that yet?'

The marshal's gaze got a little testy. 'No!'

Castle changed the subject. 'Let Nan go take care of old man Black.'

Waters arose nodding. He returned Castle to his cell, took Nan back up front with him and told her she could go. She glared. 'My paw and the others too?'

'Your paw and the two rangemen – Castle I want to hold for another day or two.'

'Why? What does it take to get an idea into your head? Tom, I know my paw's pig-headed but right now I'm beginning to think he can't hold a candle to you.'

Tom Waters's temper had been tested twice within the past hour or so. He went to the door, opened it and jerked his head. 'Out!'

Nan did not move. 'I'll stay.'

The lawman still held the door open as he stared at the woman for a moment, then slammed the door, took down his keys, opened the cell-room door and jerked his head without saying a word.

After locking her in he unlocked the cage of the two men the Humphrey boys had brought in. When they both arose the marshal said, 'Bishop! Morrison you stay.'

He herded the unwashed coarse-featured rangeman into the office, pointed to the wall bench Al Castle had recently vacated, went to his desk and leaned on it eyeing the other man.

Bishop had a low, broad forehead, a mop of unruly coarse brown hair, a wound for a mouth and bold grey eyes. He gave the lawman look for look. When Tom Waters said, 'What was the ruckus up yonder between you'n Morrison and the Humphrey boys?'

Bishop was slow answering. His gaze went to the wall-rack of rifles, shotguns and carbines with a chain run through each trigger guard and fastened at one end by a large brass lock.

Waters waited patiently, but when it appeared Bishop might not answer at all, Waters arose, picked up an ash spoke in a corner and started around from behind his desk.

Bishop's eyes widened but he continued to sit in silence until Waters was less than ten feet away, then he said, 'We figured they was stealin' them Quarter Circle R cattle. We figured to stop 'em an' drive the cattle back to where they belonged.'

Waters stood legs apart, holding the wagon spoke in both hands. 'Where did they belong?'

'We'd ask around in town. We're new in this country. Only been here a couple of weeks.'

'Where do the pair of you work?'

'We don't. This is our loafin' year.'

'Where are you from?'

'Lots of places; Idaho on the high desert, Colorado, in the Raton country. Mister, we've rode a lot of places.'

'And stolen a lot of cattle?'

Bishop straightened on the bench. 'We ain't rustlers!'

'Then how did you know those cattle were coming down from Corral Canyon?'

Bishop's eyes flicked away then back. 'We was just ridin', gettin' to know the country. We come onto those cattle by accident.'

'And lit into the Humphrey boys accusin' them of stealin' cattle when you didn't know the Humphreys or most of the stockmen in the country?' Waters retreated to his desk and perched on one corner of it. He tossed the ash spoke atop the desk as he said, 'What's your first name?'

'That's it – Bishop.'

'What's your last name?'

'Smith.'

Waters looked dourly at Bishop Smith. 'Sure it is, Smith, Jones, Brown, Black.' He sat gazing at the prisoner for a moment before saying, 'I'll tell you why you got upset when you stumbled on to the Humphreys driving those cattle – because you knew they was supposed to be penned up in that canyon – an' you knew that because you'n Morrison an' two other fellers put them there.'

'What the hell are you talkin' about?' Bishop retorted. 'Marshal, you got to have proof when you talk like that an' I can tell you – there isn't none. Not one speck.'

Waters was silent a long time before arising to herd Bishop back to his cell and lock him in as he jerked his head for Morrison to come out and be herded up to the jailhouse office and be told where to sit, which was the same place Bishop had sat.

Morrison was a larger man than Bishop, and could have been beefier if he hadn't made it a lifelong point not to exert himself if it could be avoided.

He too had coarse features. He also had the initial sprouting of a beard. He leaned forward on the bench clasping both hands and watching Marshal Waters get settled behind his desk.

The silence was broken when Waters fished forth the makings and created a brown-paper cigarette. Morrison said, 'You got any to spare?'

Waters finished, tightened two pucker strings and tossed the little sack with its papers on the back to the man on the bench. Waters lighted up watching Morrison roll a quirley. When it was finished Waters tossed a sulphur lucifer for his prisoner to light up from.

When Morrison had his cigarette trickling smoke he said, 'Obliged. I run out a couple of days back.'

The unwashed, sly-eyed prisoner relaxed. Tom Waters smoked in silence right up until he tipped ash into a tray made of metal brazed to the bottom of a horseshoe. As he did this he said, 'You fellers should have stayed in the canyon with the cattle. If you had your friends might not have got shot.'

Morrison stared. 'What are you talkin' about?'

'Did you know your friends went up there the day after the cattle was driven into that box canyon, an' found Castle already there?'

This time Morrison's gaze remained fixed and unblinkingly on Marshal Waters. Smoke trickled unheeding up his face.

Waters settled back at the desk. 'They didn't like Castle knowin' about the canyon nor the stolen cattle ... Their mistake was to think Castle was some saddlebackin' rangeman.'

Morrison said, 'What was he?'

'Fast enough to kill your friends without them getting off a shot.'

Morrison shifted on the bench shaking his head. 'I don't know about anything you've said, mister, but I'll tell you one thing – no man could shoot two men without gettin' shot himself.'

The marshal leaned, removed two six-guns from a drawer and placed them in plain sight atop his desk. 'Neither gun had been fired, Morrison ... You recognise 'em?'

' ... No. I never seen those guns before.'

'Bishop had, Morrison.'

The rumpled unwashed man eased up until his back was against the wall. He groped for a reply and found one. 'Maybe Bishop has, I never have.'

Waters said, 'You're lyin', and I don't like liars.

Bishop knew those two men the Humphreys found dead in the canyon.'

'Maybe Bishop did. You should be talkin' to him, not me.'

'I already talked to him.' Waters picked up the ash spoke. 'My persuader works every time, sometimes it's got to break bones but it works.' Waters put the spoke down and leaned on the desk.

Morrison seemed un-intimidated by the ash spoke. 'Marshal, you use that thing on folks an' they'll lie like hell not to get hit with it again.'

Waters reached into a lower drawer, produced a bottle of whiskey and said, 'You like good whiskey, Morrison? Help yourself.'

The prisoner sat across the room eyeing Waters sardonically. 'Yeah, I like whiskey, but not now.' He smiled. 'What other tricks you figure to try?'

'Just one,' replied the lawman, and arose. 'The town wants to lynch somebody. Get up.'

Morrison did not move but his sardonic expression was gone. Waters went over to stand in front of him. 'You think I won't turn you over to be lynched?'

Morrison's expression reflected uneasiness but he remained silent.

Waters leaned, caught a handful of filthy shirt and yanked the prisoner to his feet. He swung him half around and hit him when he was turning back.

Morrison fell over a bench against the west wall above which were the chained guns in their wall rack.

Waters went over, pulled Morrison to his feet

and raised his voice. 'Try to escape from my jail, will you?' and this time struck him in the soft parts.

Morrison folded over gasping at about the same time the roadway door was flung violently inward. The saloonman, Jeb Devlin, Doc Simpson and a balding storekeeper with a bull neck pushed into the room. They had been outside when the marshal had yelled about someone trying to break out of the jailhouse.

They stopped dead still. Morrison was straightening up but with painful slowness. He ignored the men in front of the open door, hurled himself at the marshal, struck Waters with a bony fist and would have struck him again but the men in the doorway bawled like wild bulls and rushed forward. They knocked Morrison down. One man gripped each arm behind Morrison's back and Jeb Devlin put a foot on Morrison's neck as he looked at the marshal. 'You all right? What'n hell happened in here? Folks could hear you bellow plumb across in front of the mercantile.' Devlin scowled downward. 'Who'n hell is he, anyway?'

Marshal Waters pointed. 'Put him on the bench. Nobody breaks out of my jail. Prop the son of a bitch up.' He paused to breathe then scowled at the townsmen as he also said, 'It wasn't just Amos Humphrey's hired riders who stole cattle, it was this man an' three of his friends. What Castle did was kill two of them in the mountains when they were goin' to kill him! Yank him to his feet. I was questionin' him when he jumped me. Open the cell room door. I'll lock him up and toss the key in the stove.'

Two townsmen helped Marshal Waters get the battered man to his cell and locked in. The third townsman, Jeb Devlin, was examining two worn, unloaded six-guns on the lawman's desk.

9
No Way Out!

Tom Waters saw the three townsmen out, closed
the door after them, went to his desk to sit gazing
at the six-guns of two dead cattle thieves. He
hadn't gotten the incriminating statement but he
had read Morrison's face correctly: Morrison had
known the stolen cattle were in Corral Canyon.
That would not get a conviction when the
circuit-riding judge arrived in town, but that
might not be for quite a while. Waters had to
think of some other way to get Bishop and
Morrison to implicate themselves.

He was sitting like that, bemused, eyeing the
six-guns in front of him when the door was flung
violently inward for the second time. Those
cattlemen who had been posse-riders stormed in.
One of them, a dried up, sinewy man named
Cunningham planted himself in front of the desk
and said, 'Why didn't you tell us them two men
you locked up before we rode with you to the Black
place was rustlers?'

Waters looked at the three angry faces when he
replied. 'Because I didn't know it. I didn't have

any idea until about half an hour ago.'

Cunningham had to accept that. He and his companions did not however, lose their hostile expressions. One of them a man named Forrest Morgan, a dark individual of average height, built like a bull, leaned to glare as he said, 'We want 'em Tom.'

Marshal Waters arose. 'Is that a fact? There won't be no lynching!'

Len Cunningham placed both hands atop the desk glaring. 'How you goin' to stop it?'

'Lock you three up if I got to.'

Cunningham made a bleak smile. 'It won't help. We sent for other stockmen an' their riders.'

Waters considered the three angry men. He'd about half got what he'd wanted from one of his prisoners. He'd thought he wouldn't have any trouble holding them until the circuit rider arrived, during which time he'd rawhide the truth from Bishop and Morrison if he had to.

Len Cunningham straightened off the desk and started around it toward the wall peg with the key ring on it. Marshal Waters turned to grab Cunningham's arm. Someone in front of the desk cocked a gun. Both Waters and Cunningham froze. The sinewy stockman looked back and smiled, shook free of the lawman and got the key ring. In front of the desk both the other stockmen had guns in their fists. Only one was cocked, but that hardly made much difference.

The marshal said, 'You'll be in trouble up to your gullets if you lynch those men.'

Cunningham sighed and wagged his head. 'Tom, it's the law – rustlers an' horse thieves hang.'

'An' what do I tell the judge when he gets here?'

'Anythin' you want to – there won't be no bodies. How'll Hizzoner feel about tryin' men that don't exist?'

Cunningham said, 'Eustis, stay here an' keep an eye on him ... Marshal, put your handgun on the desk with them other guns. *Now!*' The second man in front of the desk moved his gun. It was aimed at the lawman's soft parts.

Marshal Waters put his six-gun with the other guns and spoke quietly, reasonably, to the cattlemen. 'If you do this the sky'll fall on you. The judge will sure as hell call in federal marshals.'

Eustis Blount's hostile expression did not alter as he replied to the marshal. 'Good; they can fetch in the army too ... Tom, these two won't be the first. No one's ever found the others either. Sit down, relax. You've said your piece. Just set and be quiet.'

Cunningham and Forrest Morgan who ran cattle and horses four miles south of Campton, entered the cell room. Tom sat at his desk with Eustis watching him like a hawk. Eustis was not a bad individual. For that matter neither were the other two, but they absolutely believed in what they were doing. Nothing had changed enough to eliminate lynchings which had been going on for years. And would continue for many more years.

There was an abrupt explosion of voices down in the cell room. Most noticeable was the bull-bass of Amos Humphrey.

'Len, what in hell do you think you're doing?'

'Takin' a couple of cow thieves out to hang.'

Humphrey said no more but Avery did, he was

less vindictive than the others, exactly as he was also less bellicose. 'Mister Cunningham, how do you know them two are rustlers?'

Cunningham was busy with the key ring and the lock so Forrest Morgan replied to Avery. 'Hell, it's all over town.'

Avery replied dryly. 'You can hear anythin' in Campton if you listen long enough.'

Forrest Morgan stepped around until he could see Avery. He snarled at him. 'The Humphrey boys had trouble with those two when they was drivin' stolen cattle toward town. They're rustlers as sure as I'm a foot tall.'

Avery turned away but Al Castle took his place in front of the cell. He was no more averse to hanging rustlers than most stockmen were, but what he said did not bear directly on lynching. 'If you're wrong it'll be plain murder. I wouldn't hang anyone on town gossip.'

Forrest Morgan had heard stories about Castle too, not that he stole cattle but that he was a gunman and a killer. Morgan regarded Al Castle in a different way when he replied. 'Mister, from what I heard at the saloon you was thought to be one of 'em.'

'Then you'd better lynch me too,' Castle said, and exchanged steady looks with the cowman until Len Cunningham began to swear. 'None of these keys work in the lock ... Forrest, go back up yonder and find out if Tom has another key.'

Morgan was reluctant to break off his involvement with Castle but he returned to the office, and while he was gone something happened in the cell occupied by Bishop and Morrison. They had

been silent up to now, before Bishop spoke
through the bars to Cunningham, sounding
amused. 'The right key ain't on that ring. The
marshal put it in his pocket.'

Cunningham stood staring at Bishop, then
spun on his heel heading for the office. When he
was gone Bishop pushed up to the front of his cell
and spoke quietly to the other prisoners. 'Spit on
a piece of your handkerchief, find a splinter or
something and force the cloth into the lock. Force
it hard, don't leave no cloth showing.'

They listened but said nothing. Nan stood with
Castle at the front of the cell. 'We can't stop it.
Anyway, rustlers deserve to get lynched.' Her
voice had the ring of absolute conviction.

Castle said nothing so she gently butted him
with her shoulder. He turned slightly and stopped
breathing. In the fold of her riding skirt she was
holding an over-and-under .44 calibre Derringer.

Neither one of them spoke. They gazed steadily
at each other until the heavy footfalls of men
coming into the cell room was audible. To Castle,
from this point on events were unlikely to include
him.

Eustis remained part way up the corridor as
Cunningham and Morgan prodded Marshal
Waters ahead of them. Waters stopped in front of
the cell, inserted the key from the ring of keys,
pushed, twisted and turned, removed the key and
scowled at the men watching from inside the cell.
He spoke to Cunningham without taking his eyes
off the men inside. 'They plugged the lock. If they
used lead or something like it, you'll never get the
door open, unless you get the blacksmith.'

Cunningham was red in the face. He glared at the men inside the cell, then jerked his head. 'Eustis, take the marshal back out of here. Watch him, he's as slippery as an eel.'

Eustis did as he had been told. Cunningham said, 'Stand back, you cow stealin' bastards, I wouldn't want a ricochet to kill you.'

He was in the act of aiming his six-gun at the lock from a distance of less than six or eight feet when Forrest Morgan squawked. 'There'll be pieces of the lock flyin' in all directions.'

Len Cunningham's aggravations to this point had been overpowering. They should have the rustlers over to the saloon by now where others were waiting with hangropes.

He was raising his six-gun, thumb atop the hammer, when Nan Humphrey said, 'Drop it, Mister Cunningham. Drop it or I'll blow your head off.'

Both cattlemen turned very slowly and stared. Nan chose this moment to cock both hammers of the belly-gun. 'Let it fall, Mister Cunningham … Mister Morgan kick it over here under the door. Your's too.'

It was accomplished without anything worse than the venomous looks both stockmen put on Nan Humphrey. As Forrest Morgan was stepping back from pushing both handguns under the strap-steel door, he addressed the woman.

'Do you know what you're doing?'

Nan's little big-bored weapon was nearly lost in her hand. 'I think I do. I hope I do. Now the key ring and not a sound from any of you. The key ring, Mister Morgan.'

He did as he'd done before with the six-guns, he dropped it and used the toe of his boot to send it skittering inside the cell by way of the scant six inches between the floor and the bottom of the door.

Nan wig-wagged with the little belly-gun with its big-bore twin barrels, one above the other.

It wasn't a weapon to rely on if the distance was more than thirty yards, but in its own way it seemed a very deadly weapon, which it was.

Cunningham snarled at the woman. 'You'll never get out of town. Folks know me'n Forrest an' Eustis are down here. When you walk out of here they'll figure somethin' went wrong. They won't let you leave town.'

Morris had one of the weapons kicked under the door and was examining it. He looked up beaming. 'It's new an' got a full load. Things are lookin' up.'

Avery picked up the second gun. It was not new, but factory bluing was still in place everywhere but the protruding front sight. There, abrasion had rubbed off all the bluing. It was also fully loaded.

Nan retrieved the keys and handed them to Al Castle. He had to practically perform a contortionist's act to reach through, lift the lock and insert a key. It was the wrong one. He tried another and another, finally when he inserted and twisted it, the lock sprang open.

Bishop and his cell mate were gripping steel straps in the front of their cage. They watched the woman and her companions leave their cell. One of them, Bishop, spoke quickly. 'Let us out.'

None of the men with Nan Humphrey even glanced in their direction. Their immediate concern was the pair of cattlemen. Morris gestured with one of the appropriated six-guns for the stockmen to walk up to the office, which they did.

Because Eustis Blount was sitting against the north wall on a bench, his preferred position for watching Marshal Waters, he did no more than glance up when Morgan and Cunningham came out of the cell room, but Tom Waters, sitting where he could see behind the first men to emerge could also see behind them. He did not move nor make a sound.

Eustis was leaning to arise when Morris emerged and pointed one of the six-guns at him. Eustis seemed to turn to stone as he leaned.

Len Cunningham glared at the marshal. 'She had a belly-gun. Don't you search 'em before lockin' 'em up!'

Tom Waters had both hands atop the table where the two empty guns were lying. He ignored Cunningham's caustic remark.

Amos was a willing follower of his daughter, but clearly not a happy one. He had thought of the consequences and did not like what his mind told him.

He nevertheless went over to retrieve his shotgun and Colt.

Morris told Avery and Forrest Morgan to go get the horses and tie them outside the jailhouse. Avery did not like that arrangement. 'Morris all he's got to do is yell … I'll go alone.'

Marshal Waters finally spoke, but not until

Avery was gone. He looked squarely at Amos. 'Do you know what you're doing? You're goin' to lose everything you own. You'll be an outlaw.'

The older man fidgetted, shifted his shotgun from one hand to the other and looked at his daughter. She answered the lawman without looking at her father.

'Why did you let those lynchers in here? You want Al hanged too, don't you?'

'No! They walked in like folks do every day. I didn't have any idea what they were up to ... Give me those keys ... I'll lock them in an' hold 'em until hell freezes over an' for two days on the ice.' Waters held out his hand, Nan made no move to give him the keys until Castle bumped her and nodded his head.

Waters stood up angry, motioned for the stockmen to precede him and locked them in. None of them spoke. As the lawman was turning away he put a sulphurous glare on his new prisoners, returned to the office, flung the keys atop his desk and addressed Amos again. 'You're puttin' everything you own on the block for two lousy cow thieves.' He remained standing in front of the closed cell room door glaring at the older man.

There was noise out front. Morris eased the door a few inches before saying the horses were outside and moved back as Avery pushed past him.

Avery, usually reflective and calm, was agitated. 'They're out front of the saloon. About ten of 'em.'

'Who?' Waters asked.

'Cowmen! They watched me lead the horses down here. They was millin' an' talkin'. They'll come down here sure as hell.'

Tom Waters sighed, returned to his desk but remained standing behind it. 'Amos ...?'

The large older man sank down on the bench where the racked weapons were chained. He leaned the shotgun aside and looked at his daughter in an accusing way, but he ignored the marshal.

Even Morris was finally having bad second thoughts. He had felt triumphant when he walked out of the cell with the others. Now, the more he dwelt on their situation the more his normally self confident attitude wilted.

Amos finally spoke. 'Let 'em have 'em. They deserve a lynchin' anyway.'

His daughter reminded him of something else. 'They'll want *three* men to hang, paw.'

Amos looked at Al Castle, gave his head a slight wag and returned to studying the toes of his boots.

Marshal Waters spoke quietly. 'Put the guns on my desk. I'll go up yonder and talk to the cowmen. They can have Bishop and Morrison. What happened in here only we know. It'd be best if none of us ever talked about Nan usin' a belly-gun to get you out.' He looked gravely at the woman. 'They got no grudge against the rest of you.'

' ... Al Castle?' she said, returning the lawman's gaze without blinking.

Waters hung fire. He had no good answer. The stockmen surely had heard about Castle. In their present mood they'd want him too. 'If they'll listen, I'll explain about Castle. He wasn't one of the rustlers.'

Avery was watching the lawman when he said, 'Will they take your word, Marshal?'

'I don't know. In the past they have.'

Avery wagged his head. 'Marshal, from what I saw out there – they're goin' to hold a lynchin' an' if they think Castle needs hangin' too, they'll string him up with the others.'

There was a slight commotion outside in the roadway. Men called back and forth. One particular man out front of the saloon called very distinctly. 'I wouldn't go in there if I was you boys.'

If there was a reply it could not be made out in the jailhouse. Nan pushed past Avery and cracked the door a few inches. Her tired body straightened, she smiled and moved aside for her brothers to enter.

Martin and Pete Humphrey stopped cold. They saw their slumped and demoralised father across the room on the bench, saw the others, dirty, rumpled, clearly under terrific strain and lastly looked at their sister. She alone of the people in the room was smiling.

Marshal Waters neither nodded nor spoke although he knew the old man's sons well.

Avery sighed. 'Two more an' I'm hungry enough to chew the rear end out of a bear if someone'd hold its head.' Morris perked up a little. The old man's boys stood near the door looking bewildered until Nan started at the beginning and told them the entire story, from start to finish. It took time. Outside one man called and another answered.

Avery said, 'I told you – they're comin'.'

10
Choices

Martin Humphrey looked like his father, was built like him and when he spoke he sounded like him. 'There's enough guns on the wall rack … How you fixed for ammunition, Tom?'

Waters rolled his eyes. 'Martin, we couldn't make it work. All they got to do is stand around and wait.'

The youngest Humphrey was close to his sister when he spoke. 'They want those fellers we brought in? Let 'em have 'em. From what Nan just said they're cow thieves.'

Tom Waters looked almost pityingly at Pete Humphrey. 'They'll want Castle too.'

Martin looked at his sister. She nodded her head. Martin then said, 'All right, Nan. You'n Castle go out the back way, down to the liverybarn, get two horses and head for the ranch. We'll let them inside, let them have the rustlers, and that'll keep 'em occupied.'

Castle was listening. When Martin finished he looked at his sister. She almost imperceptibly nodded at him. Martin went over to sit beside his

father. He ignored everyone else. 'You all right?'
he asked. The older man barely shook his head
while looking at his daughter. 'Suppose they'll be
around back?'

Morris went through a storeroom, cracked the
alley door and stood a long time before closing the
door and returning to the office where he said, 'If
they're back there, they're invisible. All I saw was
a rat-tailed dog pokin' among the trash barrels.'

Waters gazed at Martin and his father. They
ignored him. Avery was leaning against the wall
as solemn as an owl. Only Morris showed life; it
was his nature to be optimistic.

Nan bumped Castle and led the way through
the storeroom. Before opening the door she
turned. 'The barn's a fair walk. Someone will
certainly see us walking down the alley.'

He believed that. 'As long as it's not lynchers …
Nan?'

'What.'

'I meant it.'

She stood a long moment regarding Castle,
eventually turned to lift the door-bar and slowly
open it wide enough for two people to emerge.

A woman across the alley was standing beside a
mounded clothes basket from which she selected
pieces to be hanged from a lass-rope clothesline.
Otherwise Nan saw nothing to worry about.

She whispered to Al as she stepped outside. The
woman across the alley saw her and waved, then
turned her back as she leaned to take a heavy wet
sheet, flip it a couple of times before flinging it
across the rope which ran from the rear of a house
to the only tree in the woman's yard.

Castle had Nan Humphrey on his right side. They had to pass several vacant areas between buildings. Although loud voices were audible around front in the vicinity of the jailhouse, the farther they walked the fewer people were visible out on the main thoroughfare and the less noise they heard.

Castle said, 'Faster.'

Nan widened her stride. They did not speak until they were between the rear livery barn entrance and a large old cribbed pole corral across the alley.

Not often but occasionally Fate was kind to people; the liveryman was not in his barn. He was over in front of the emporium watching cattlemen in front of the jailhouse. He wasn't the only one, it seemed half the town was over there, men, women and youngsters.

The stockmen used pistol butts to hammer on the jailhouse door. They loudly demanded that Marshal Waters open up.

Inside, Avery went through the store room to close and bar the alley door from the inside, then, on his return he also closed the store room door.

An angry cowman called for his companions to be quiet, then asked if Marshal Waters could hear him. The marshal said he could. The cowman allowed a moment to pass then called back that he and his companions were going to shoot the hinges off the door.

Waters looked at the tense people in the room before he called back. 'The first man through that door will get blown to hell. We got shotguns in here and plenty of rounds.'

Another stockman called out. Those inside who
recognised the voice stated a name. 'Will Rowe.'
Marshal Waters nodded. Will Rowe was a horse
and mule rancher southeast of town. He was
known as a violent, belligerent individual. He
said, 'Tom ... I got three sticks of dynamite left
over from blowin' stumps at home.'

They waited for more but Rowe said no more.
Avery sagged down on a bench. Tom Waters said,
'They're crazy.' Avery looked up at the lawman.
'You know what just one stick of blastin' powder
will do to this building?'

Amos listened to something his son said, then
spoke to Tom Waters. 'Nan'n Castle had plenty of
time. Let 'em in.'

The others nodded in agreement. Waters went
to the door but did not lift the bar until he'd
spoken to the men outside one last time. It was an
attempt to buy Castle and Amos's daughter a
little more time. He said, 'All right, I'll open the
door, but if you take those men out of here an'
hang 'em, everyone in here will be able to testify
who each of you are.'

Rowe's growl came back. 'Just open the damned
door. We'll take our chances. There's no judge in
this territory who'll decide against us, but if there
is – you won't have no bodies. *Open the damned
door!*'

Marshal Waters lifted the *tranca*. The cowmen
charged in guns drawn. Waters was struck by the
violently flung-back door. Amos and his son on the
west-wall bench recognised every man who
rushed inside. Avery and Morris recognised
several but not all. Tom Waters also knew every

man. Rowe was a beefy individual with nearly snow-white hair. He wore glasses behind which pale blue eyes glared. He said, 'The keys to the cells!'

Marshal Waters pointed. Rowe grabbed the keys, hurled back the cell room door and stalked down the narrow corridor. He was followed by all but two stockmen. Their attention was caught and held by Len Cunningham, who had sat like a statue throughout everything up until now. He said, 'Amos's girl an' that feller called Castle went out the back door to get horses at the livery barn.'

A loud commotion in the cell room held everyone's attention who was not down there. Men were swearing, the sound of blows, scuffling and cursing filled the corridor and reached up into the office.

When Bishop and Morrison were kicked, punched and prodded into the office their shirts were torn, they had bruises and glared at the marshal as they cursed him.

Will Rowe punched Morrison toward the door. Several men had to drag the fighting, swearing, twisting and turning man known as Bishop. It was more a melee than a struggle. The rustlers kicked, spat, twisted violently to free themselves of strong hands. They lunged with bared teeth.

If it had been an equal manhandling Waters felt fairly certain Bishop and Morrison might have broken loose.

Now, with the weight of rock-hard cattlemen fighting to control the outlaws, it was simply a matter of time. The first renegade to concede was Morrison, who lacked the toughness and resolution of Bishop.

Eventually, probably the result of exhaustion, both outlaws gave up, stopped struggling and stopped swearing.

The stockmen got a respite, which several of them needed. Will Rowe stood wide-legged regarding the rustlers. He glared through a brief moment of silence, then with hands on his hips addressed the others.

'Hangin's too good for 'em. I think tying their arms behind their backs, then lashin' them to a couple of cantles an' hittin' the horses would be better.'

No one responded favourably to this idea. Rowe grabbed Bishop and hurled him out of the jailhouse, came up behind him and dragged him across the road in the direction of the saloon where other rangemen were waiting, one of them with two hang-ropes complete with expertly fashioned slip knots draped from a shoulder.

All the rangemen but two, Len Cunningham and Forrest Morgan, left the jailhouse, and those two turned on the others including the town marshal. Morgan was equally as furious as his companion but because Cunningham had a quicker and more vitriolic tongue, Morgan remained silent.

Cunningham glared at the marshal. 'You think you're clever, lettin' Amos's girl an' that other cow thief get away … Well, that wasn't clever at all because Forrest and I're goin' to get a few others an' go after 'em.'

Waters stood in front of his desk giving look for look with the stockman. 'Get it through your thick skull, Len, Castle wasn't one of 'em.'

'Well, I think he was. Forrest ...?'

Morgan nodded his head but did not speak. Cunningham looked malevolently at the lawman. 'Tom, you done somethin' that's inexcusable – you tried to keep us from gettin' them rustlers. Folks'll remember that.'

Waters's reply was quietly given. It was in notable contrast with all the previous shouting and scuffling. He said, 'Len, leave it be. Castle wasn't one of 'em, so don't make it any worse'n it already is.'

Cunningham glared around the room, jerked his head for Morgan to follow, and led the way out of the jailhouse, but he did not cross the road and walk northward in the direction of the saloon, he walked southward in the direction of the livery barn where he had stabled his horse shortly after arriving in town.

Tom Waters sank down at his desk. When Pete Humphrey arose to leave he hesitated long enough to say he was going to try and reach his sister and Castle before the ranchers did. Martin hung fire, troubled about going with his brother or remaining behind with his father. Amos said, 'He'll need help, Martin.'

The older man's eldest son nodded, left the jailhouse and Marshal Waters went over to close the door without bothering to bar it. From over there he considered Amos Humphrey. 'Care for a jolt?' The cowman nodded so Waters got his bottle from the lower drawer of his desk, handed the bottle to the large older man, took it back, stoppered it and put it back in the drawer.

He rolled and lighted a smoke, considered the

older man and said, 'Nothin' worse than a lynch
mob. A man might as well talk to a rock.'

Amos remained speechless but he solemnly
nodded his head.

There was no attempt made to mute the noise
from the saloon. There was a fierce and loud
argument up there between Jeb Devlin and the
lynchers. The latter wanted to hang Bishop and
Morrison from the fir crown-piece of the saloon's
ceiling. The proprietor was loudly profane and
adamant that this would not be done. He told
them to do their hanging among the scattering of
trees east or west of town.

In retrospect Marshal Waters would reflect on
how ridiculous that argument was – except that
stockmen had undoubtedly been drinking before
arriving out front of his jailhouse.

The silence was broken when Amos asked for
another taste from the bottle. Waters handed it
over, counted the number of times the older man's
adam's apple bobbed up and down, took back the
bottle and stowed it away.

Amos's gaze sharpened, he straightened on the
bench. 'I'd best go hunt up the boys an' Nan ... I've
known Len Cunningham a long time, an' I can tell
you for a fact, when he gets as fired up as he is
today, he don't think straight. Hell, he don't think
at all.'

After the older man departed Marshal Waters
stood in his roadway door listening. The argument
at the saloon had been settled. He gazed at the
empty tie-rack in that part of town, closed the
door at his back and walked across the roadway,
turned northward and pushed into an empty

saloon where the scent of tobacco smoke and spilt liquor made a pleasant combination.

Jeb Devlin leaned on his bar watching the lawman cross toward him. Before Waters could speak the saloonman said, 'They wanted to lynch them two outlaws in my saloon … You look like you need a little stiffenin'.' Devlin brought a bottle and two small glasses back with him. He poured both glasses full, shoved the bottle aside and made a mock salute with his upraised glass while looking Tom Waters squarely in the eye.

'Here's to hell an' them as goes there.'

Waters did not touch his glass. 'Where did they take 'em?'

Devlin made an exaggerated gesture with both outflung arms. 'I didn't ask an' they didn't say.' He dropped his arms, put his head slightly to one side and asked a question.

'Do you figure it's wrong?'

Tom finally raised his little glass, dropped its contents straight down and shook his head.

Devlin looked relieved. 'Someday, maybe fifty or a hunnert years from now, folks'll stumble on to a couple of graves. By then there won't be anyone around who remembers.'

Waters faintly frowned. 'Is that good, Jeb?'

'I got no idea whether it's good or not, all I know is that there'll be two less worthless sons of bitches around … Care for a refill?'

'No thanks.' Waters turned to depart. Devlin had one more question for him.

'Are you plumb satisfied that Castle feller wasn't one of 'em?'

'I'm as sure as day follows night.'

'Well, somethin' I can tell you. When some of
'em finish with the hangings they figure to hunt
that feller up ... Tom, they've still got lynching in
mind.'

Waters returned to his jailhouse. To pass time
he swept out, cleaned up his office, dropped those
two empty guns from the top of his desk into a
drawer, made certain the alley door had been
barred from inside, and eventually, with the town
quiet again, leaned in his roadway door to roll and
light a smoke.

Across the road women with mesh bags entered
and left the emporium. Except for an almost
solemn silence, Campton seemed normal. He went
down to the livery barn where the proprietor saw
him enter from the roadway, and flung both arms
wide.

Marshal Waters sank down on a bench outside
the harness room. 'How about the others?'

'What others?'

'The ranchers, damn it.'

'Oh them – well, they took their animals with
'em, tied them two whinin' outlaws on behind and
rode out of town around through the east side
alley. Beyond that I got no idea. But if they didn't
return to town, why then I'd guess they went
home ... They done all they come to town to do,
didn't they?'

Waters didn't answer. He left the livery barn,
entered his spanking-clean jailhouse office, propped both feet atop the desk and stared at the far
wall. It was a long day, he had no visitors and
wondered if that wasn't because folks disapproved
of him handing over two men to lynchers.

One of the really genuine flaws with human nature was that people willingly believed the first tale told them. Later, when this was proven wrong, they still believed it. The solution was to tell the first lie.

Tom Waters hadn't had the chance. The deed was done before he could even leave the jailhouse. He started to reach for his tobacco sack, changed his mind and leaned to retrieve the whiskey bottle from a lower desk drawer, take two healthy swallows and put the bottle back.

Much later Doctor Simpson came by. Doc had cigar ash down his vest and although his coat and trousers matched, both were rumpled. Doc said, 'I just came back from lookin' in on Elijah.' Doc wagged his head. 'He wasn't there.' At the lawman's quizzical look Doc said more. 'There was tracks of a light wagon enterin' the yard from the west, makin' a big sashay from in front of the house then goin' back the way it came.'

'Where was Avery and Morris?'

'I got no idea. There wasn't a soul on the place.' Doc clasped both hands across his middle and scowled at the stove as he said, 'I came back ... I could have shagged those buckboard tracks but it was gettin' along and I don't like missin' supper.' Simpson's shrewd eyes went to the lawman. 'Who's west of Elijah's yard?'

Tom Waters finally understood. 'The Humphrey place ... Someone came, got Elijah an' took him over there with them?'

Doctor Simpson re-settled more comfortably where he sat before speaking. 'On the ride back I figured a theory. Care to hear it?'

'Shoot.'

'They had that Castle-feller with 'em. And Nan. I figure those two stopped off to see how old Elijah was making out on their way to the Humphrey place. They went on home, got a rig an' came back to haul Elijah to the Humphrey place. That way Nan could look after the old billy goat an' ...'

'And?'

'Her paw, brothers, Elijah's two riders an' that Castle-feller could fort up.' Simpson leaned to arise. 'From what I heard durin' your stand-off with the stockmen – Nan and that Castle-feller got away, headed west – well – that'd fit in with the rest of my theory. They got the old screwt, took him....'

'You already said that, Doc.'

Simpson arose nodding. 'For a fact I already said that ... Where are the ranchers, Tom?'

After Doctor Simpson left Marshal Waters sat a while in thought. Eventually, he groaned and arose. The last thing he felt up to was the long saddleback ride to the Humphrey place, and, the powerful suspicion that it would be a fruitless ride; if the cowmen had gone home as the liveryman had surmised, fine, but if they had decided to hunt down Nan and Al Castle they'd have a fair idea where to find them.

Providing Amos, his boys and the pair of Elijah Black riders were forted up with the Humphreys, along with Amos's daughter and Al Castle, this time it might end differently.

He got his horse and rode west with a slight northerly angle. Half way along he remembered not having eaten recently and tried to fill the void with a smoke. Usually this was an exercise in futility, but he did it anyway.

It hadn't occurred to him to make up a posse as he'd done the last time he rode westerly from town, and when the idea came, instinct told him he would have failed. The other time excepting the rangemen, his posse-riders hadn't been enthusiastic. This time, since they would have all been townsmen, he most likely would have heard some of the most artful excuses under the sun.

It would be dusk before he reached the Black yard and even darker by the time he arrived at the Humphrey place. While he dawdled at Elijah's yard hopeful of finding Morris and Avery, dusk unnoticeably became early nightfall. He grained his horse in the barn, sat in one of the chairs under the bunkhouse overhang and waited. No one rode into the yard. He went inside, found some cold corned beef hash, ate half of it, got his animal and doggedly headed westerly again.

Riding into someone's yard after nightfall wasn't prudent; doing it when the people would be forted up expecting trouble, was something less than wise.

He saw the lights more than a mile before he got close enough for the Humphrey dogs to pick up his scent and set up a chorus that would have put a pack of wolves to shame.

He watched the main-house and bunkhouse. When the barking was at its peak the lights in both those places were blanked out.

Waters sighed, but his horse had both ears sideways and his head down. He disliked even quiet dogs, but what was coming out of the darkness was a pack of dogs. He had kicked his share of dogs and had struck others. He wasn't fearful, he was ready and willing.

Waters swore at the dogs, only the timid ones were sufficiently intimidated to run for cover beneath the main-house, the other three or four stood their ground, hackles up, fangs bared. Waters rode on a loose rein directly toward them. One dog fled, another shifted ground but two big male dogs did not yield an inch.

Waters rode slightly to one side of them. When they were off to one side still snarling, the marshal's horse did not turn his head but one of the male dogs was hurled ten feet and lit down whimpering and fleeing. That was too much for the second dog. He also fled for shelter under the main-house.

11
The Crisis

The marshal tied up out front of the barn, dawdled as he did this and was not surprised when a voice he recognised as belonging to one of Elijah's riders, the one named Avery, spoke quietly from the pitch-black interior of the barn.

'Marshal, are you alone?'

'Yes.'

'You're sure you didn't leave some others out yonder?'

Tom answered brusquely. 'I told you I'm alone!'

Avery hesitated. '... Come into the barn. I'll take you to the house from around in back.'

Waters left the horse tied, entered the barn where he couldn't see his hand in front of his face and hesitated only until Elijah's rider gave him directions. 'Walk in the middle of the runway an' out back. Don't stop. Turn left and keep behind the outbuildings until we reach the yard ... Marshal?'

'What.'

'I got nothin' against you. Just do like I said.'

Tom did exactly as Elijah's rider had told him to

do. When he was beyond the barn he turned
toward the next outbuilding. He could hear Avery
behind him. When they ran out of sheltering
outbuildings with open ground for several
hundred feet ahead toward the main-house porch,
a second voice speaking from darkness said, 'Who
is it, Avery?'

'Marshal Waters.'

The second man growled. 'Go to the porch steps
an' stop.'

Again the lawman obeyed. At the porch the trio
was challenged by a harsh voice. 'Morris? Avery?
What you got?'

'Marshal Waters from town.'

'Is he alone?'

'He said he come alone.'

Big Martin Humphrey arose from the porch
floor and squinted. He had a sidearm but did not
draw it. 'Tom?'

'Yes.'

'Where are the others?'

'I got no idea. After they took Bishop and
Morrison they didn't come back to town.'

Martin's reply was practical. 'They'll be along
come daylight. Come up on to the porch.'

Inside, there were two lighted lamps. The
reason he had been unable to see them earlier was
because someone had covered the windows with
blankets.

Pete, Al Castle and Nan were in the parlour.
They looked quizzically at the marshal. Pete
spoke first. 'If you made the ride out this far from
town it's got to be because the ranchers are
coming.'

Waters sank into a chair. 'I didn't see anyone on the ride out. I waited at Elijah's place. When no one showed up I came over here. If they'd been out there, I'd have heard 'em.'

Martin left the room, was gone during the interrogation and returned. He addressed the lawman. 'Elijah wants to see you.' Martin jerked his head toward a dingy hallway.

Waters remained seated. 'Is he all right?'

Martin looked at his sister, who replied to the lawman. 'He's no worse, but Al and I came on home to get a light rig and bring him back with us. He'd been drinking whiskey which he shouldn't touch. At least until he's better than he is right now.'

Waters still did not leave the chair. He looked at each of them in turn. Pete offered him a bottle from a table where old Amos had left it. Waters asked where their paw was. Martin answered from over by the hallway entrance. 'In there with Elijah ... Did they lynch those cow thieves?'

'As far as I know they did. Come daylight maybe we can find 'em in a tree.'

Martin slowly shook his head. 'No one'll ever find those two.'

Morris went to the table where Amos had left the bottle, briefly tipped it, made a loud noise expelling breath and left the bottle where he'd found it. He looked at Nan. 'Did you finish in the kitchen?'

She did not answer, she turned and went back where she had been preparing a meal. The scents of cooking reminded the lawman how famished he was. He finally arose and went toward the dark hallway, down it until he heard voices, and stopped in a bedroom doorway where a small lamp was alight on a table at bedside. Elijah saw him. 'Amos's been tellin' me what happened in town … Did they hang those sons of bitches?'

Waters entered the room shaking his head and looking for something to sit on. Amos had the only chair at bedside. Tom had to settle on some kind of cabinet; it looked like a sea chest.

'I don't know whether they hung them or not. All I know is that I waited for them to come back, an' they didn't. The liveryman thought that after hangin' Bishop and Morrison they all went home.'

Amos gazed dispassionately at Marshal Waters. 'Maybe they went home. I expect most likely they did. But they'll show up tomorrow. We got Castle an' they'll have a rope for him.'

'Amos,' the lawman replied, sounding almost like a parent reprimanding a child. 'Castle wasn't one of them.'

'He says he wasn't. Maybe it's the truth. All the same….'

Waters was tired, hungry and unhappy. He interrupted the older man. 'Amos, you can take his word. There won't be anyone left to back him up … Just for the hell of it, believe him. I do.'

Elijah wiggled under his blankets, 'So do I!'

Amos turned on Elijah. 'Hell, you scarcely more'n met Castle. You don't know a damned fact about what happened.'

Elijah flared up. 'The hell I don't. Your daughter told me. You want to call your own daughter a liar?'

Amos shot up out of the chair abruptly and

stamped out of the room. Elijah listened to his
diminishing footfalls as he wagged his head at Tom
Waters. 'He's always been like that. The only way
you could convince him a rock is a rock is by hitting
him in the head with it ... Come over on the chair,
the light's pretty weak where you're setting.'

Tom Waters and Elijah talked for a while. When
there were long lulls the marshal left Elijah, who
had a bottle under his blankets, nipped on it, re-hid
it, stretched out and went to sleep.

In the kitchen men were making desultory
conversation and eating. Nan called him to the
table, watched him eat and while her back was to
the table, rolled her eyes.

Hungry men turned drowsy after gorging themselves. Avery volunteered to keep watch in the
parlour with the light turned low so the others
could sleep.

Marshal Waters watched them drift away from
the parlour one at a time. He was the last to go. He
found an unused bedroom whose door had been
closed a long time. When he opened it chill, stale
air greeted him. There were two beds, one against
each wall. He chose the one nearest the window,
opened it a crack and was rolling in when Morris
arrived grumbling about Martin snoring like a
shoat caught under a gate. The marshal grunted,
ignored the other man and rolled up on to his side
near the barely-open window. He was normally a
sound sleeper. That propensity should have been
reinforced by the prodigious meal he had eaten,
and it probably would have been if the voices that
awakened him hadn't been close.

He listened, rose to see if Morris also heard

them, sank back down because Morris was breathing with a loug, rasping cadence. Nothing had awakened him.

A man said, 'I told you – I meant it.'

There was only one woman on the Humphrey place; it wasn't difficult recognising her voice when she replied to the man. 'You're grateful is all.'

He sounded slightly irritated when next he spoke. 'Grateful! All right, maybe a little, but you're a real handsome woman ... Quit arguin', please. I got a right to my opinion ... Nan, give me your hand.'

Evidently she gave it. Tom Waters could see neither of them in the dark beyond the window. 'Al ...'

'Yes.'

'Elijah's going to be all right. Not like he once was but good enough. I doubt he'll be able to ride. I think he's lost some of his sense of balance.'

'He's got a top buggy, Nan. I saw it in his buggy shed. He can go anywhere the land's not too steep.'

She seemed to ponder that, and eventually sounded less gloomy when she told him he was right. The trick was going to be to get the old devil to use the buggy. 'He's been a horseman, a rider, ever since I remember him as a little girl,' she told Castle.

Evidently Al Castle felt the subject of Elijah and his infirmities had gone as it had to go, because he made another personal remark.

'I was proud of you today. No one handled themselves better'n you did at the jailhouse ... You stuck up for me like we was kin.'

She did not comment immediately. When she did

the eavesdropper behind the window thought she sounded uncomfortable or embarrassed.

'I owed you,' she said.

Castle's reply to that was also slow coming. His voice was softer when he said, 'You didn't owe me, Nan. You paid that off by bringin' the water and helpin' me get back … Nan, about that damned dodger …'

'Yes.'

'I did steal four horses up in the Montana-strip country close to Wyoming.'

'Paw believes that.'

Castle hesitated again, ' … Well …?'

'Why did you do it, Al?'

'I worked eight months for a Dutchman named Nauter. He didn't pay me. I spent most of the ridin' season in a line camp. He said he was too busy at the home place to make the trip, and, anyway what good was money to someone as isolated as I was. At the end of the season he took his family, went down to Denver for the winter, paid two men to winter-feed an' left without paying the other two riders. I was one of them … So him an' I picked out four horses each and struck out. I got no idea what happened to him but those fellers Nauter left to winter feed told the sheriff I'd stolen four horses … I rode due south, sold the horses just above the Wyoming line on my way south, got almost as much for them as the damned Dutchman owed me, an' saw a Wanted dodger on me in a little town where I figured to find work, headed south into the mountains and never stopped to more'n rest my horse an' eat until I wandered into that Corral Canyon.'

Tom Waters flopped on to his back, put both arms under his head and listened. He was too interested to feel as sleepy as he'd felt earlier.

Nan had a question for Castle. 'Will that sheriff up yonder come after you?'

Castle sounded matter-of-fact when he said, 'He's a fat man. Folks up there complained that he never left town even in good weather. I doubt that he'll even follow up on them dodgers, but all the same....'

'Why don't you change your name?'

Tom Waters was interested in this question, which had puzzled him. The answer Castle gave annoyed the marshal. It sounded more than ridiculous, it sounded naive.

'I'm not an outlaw. I never used another name in my life ... Nan? I like this country, like some of the people in it. I figured I might stay. After I met you I knew I wanted to stay.'

She surprised the town marshal when she said, 'I want you to stay, Al.'

There was a long pause. Waters reared up in the bed but Castle and Amos's daughter had moved out of sight. The last thing he heard was when Castle said, 'Did you really hit a man for doing what we just did?'

Her answer was too muted. Waters sank back down looking at the ceiling, of which he could make out very little.

The following morning someone put the coffee on to boil while it was still dark. Morris awakened, looked across the room where Waters was sound asleep, threw back some quilts and stamped into his boots. That noise awakened the lawman. He too rolled out. Voices came from the vicinity of the kitchen, Waters ignored them to go out back and sluice off. When he returned Amos Humphrey was sitting at the kitchen table having his first cup of java for the day. He regarded Marshal Waters owlishly, grunted and told Martin to fetch another cup of coffee. There was no sign of Al Castle or the old man's daughter.

Pete came in from forking feed to livestock in the barn area. He had shaved, which neither his brother or father had done. Martin got two more cups of coffee, one for his brother. As Pete sat down he said, 'Quiet out there.'

Amos looked over the rim of his raised cup. 'They'll be along,' and scowled. 'Where the hell is Nan?'

She appeared in the doorway, looked at her father, went to the stove to shoulder Martin aside and got busy preparing breakfast.

The last of them to arrive was Al Castle. Morris and Avery looked up from their meal but neither Martin nor his father did until Castle took an empty chair, smiled at Nan when she brought him coffee and a plate, then said, 'I figured last night ... The only reason the cowmen'll come today is because of me.' He paused, the men kept on eating. They listened but Nan turned from over by the stove looking straight at Castle. He said the rest of it without returning her stare. 'It's not worth makin' enemies over; maybe gettin' someone shot ... Amos, I'd like to borrow a horse. Mine can't do it without shoes. I'll pay you for the horse as soon as I get a job somewhere ... Maybe, if I ride due south they won't see me. Not if they come from over near Campton.'

Amos stopped chewing. Martin pushed back his plate and looked stonily at Castle. Morris and Avery sipped coffee in silence. Pete Humphrey broke the silence. 'You got to stop runnin' sometime. You got friends here. Cunningham an' the others won't make a fight of it with us forted up an' them out in the open.'

Castle's answer was brusque. 'Whether they make a fight of it or not, Pete, what's the use? I can't stay here. The whole countryside'll be....'

Nan broke in from over by the stove. She told Pete to go get the Wanted dodger. He did not move, nor did his brother. Avery and Morris sat big-eyed. Amos arose, left the room, returned with the dodger and handed it to his daughter, knowing what she intended to do, and she did it, she rolled up the dodger, opened the firebox of the stove and shoved it into the flames.

Only Elijah's riders looked nonplussed, they hadn't known about the dodger. Amos returned to his chair, sat down and leaned until he could see Morris and Avery. 'We'd take it kindly if you never saw no Wanted poster an' never heard that Mister Castle was on it.'

Avery inclined his head while staring across the table. Morris made an elaborate wide swing of both arms. 'I never seen no dodger, an' I never heard this talk.' He grinned at Al Castle.

Amos and his eldest son were still and expressionless. For the old man, watching his daughter burn the poster was hard; he had spent his life on the side of justice – not book-law-justice. He had participated in his share of lynchings of cattle and horse thieves.

Martin, sitting beside the old man, and a spitting image of him even in the way he thought and spoke, also stared at Castle. It was Nan who broke the hush. She told them what Al Castle had told her last night. As she spoke Marshal Waters went back to eating. Amos caught him between mouthfuls. 'You believe that story, Tom?'

Waters looked straight at the old man and said, 'I'm satisfied, Amos. Maybe book-law wouldn't be; takin' horses without permission of the owner is against the law. But I'd have done the same an' so would you.'

Martin leaned back off the table gazing at the town marshal. 'I'd say Castle was justified. But that ain't our problem right now. It's Len an' Forrest an' the others. *They* won't believe it in spades.'

Al Castle nodded his head. 'I got to ride, gents, and soon; it'll be daylight directly. I'd like to get clear of the Campton country before daylight if I can.'

Nan said, 'No!' in such a loud voice the men twisted to look at her. She ignored them, all but Al Castle. 'Last night I told you I didn't want you to leave.... If you're going, I'll go with you.'

This startled everyone at the table except Castle. He looked up at her. 'It wouldn't be any life for you, Nan, duckin' an' hidin', always movin', never bein' able to put down roots.'

She was white in the face, her eyes were large, her expression was unrelenting. Martin looked at his father. Amos was staring at his daughter until he slowly faced around and considered Al Castle across the table. He was too dumbfounded to speak.

Morris arose, went to the parlour and leaned to look out the window. Dawn was close but visibility was still very limited. He went out to the porch to listen, heard nothing and returned in time to hear Martin Humphrey. 'Nan, come outside with me.' Martin pushed his chair back and arose. His sister ignored him as she addressed her father. 'Paw, we'll need two horses. I'll take grub along.'

Martin reddened. 'I said come outside with me, Nan.'

She swung to face the large man, eyes flashing. 'You've bossed me since we was children. You always knew best ... Martin, you can go to hell! I'm old enough. I know my own mind ... Paw, two horses!'

Amos was frozen in place. He had seen his daughter's temper before but never against the family. Avery and Morris were wooden-faced. They seemed to be scarcely breathing. Avery looked into his coffee cup. Morris had both hands in his lap; he was too embarrassed to move nor speak. Womenfolk did not flare out like that at menfolk. Morris was more than surprised, he was shocked. If they did flare up it was never in front of others.

The silence ran on. Amos cleared his throat and reached for his cup. It was empty. He held it as though unsure what to do with it. Nan got the pot from the stove, roughly shouldered Martin aside, refilled her father's cup, returned the pot to the stove, removed her apron and repeated what she'd said earlier, 'We need two horses, paw. It'll be daylight in another hour or so.'

Amos raised his gaze to Al Castle. Whether he intended to speak or not Martin addressed Al Castle in a cold tone of voice.

'You been meddlin' with my sister?'

Castle did not arise from the table but he put both hands on the wooden arms of the chair when he answered. 'Ask your sister!'

Martin did not take his eyes off Castle. 'I'm beginnin' to wonder if we done right takin' your side.'

Castle arose slowly. Amos came alive. 'Leave it be, Martin.'

'Paw, he....'

'Gawddamn you, *leave it be*! Set down!'

Martin sat. His father had never before sworn at him.

Nan spoke again, this time to Castle. 'Come along, I know which horses.'

Amos raised one arm. 'Nan!'

She turned on her father as she'd turned on her brother. 'What?'

'Stay. Don't go outside. Daylight's comin'. If they're out there they'll see you. It's too late.' The old man dropped his arm, sat gazing at his daughter – and softly smiled. They had always been close, more so after the death of Nan's mother. 'I didn't expect nothin' like this.' He swung his gaze to Al Castle. 'Pete was right, you got to stop runnin'. Relax, they're not goin' to get you.'

Castle answered quietly, 'Mister Humphrey, if I stay there'll never be anythin' but trouble for you – and for me.'

The old man did not relent. 'Set down. Finish

your coffee. We'll ponder on this … Nan, Mister
Castle's cup is empty.'

12
The Riders From Town

The sun arrived and massively climbed. Marshal Waters had left early when it was still dark. Avery and Morris, uncomfortable about the way things were going, went down to the barn. Martin sat stone-faced. Only the youngest son did not act gloomy or troubled. He smiled at his sister. 'If you're hell bent on goin', maybe tonight, but not this morning. Riders would stand out clear as can be ... They'd run you down.'

Once the sun soared it was indeed too late. Amos struggled to his feet, jerked his head for Martin to follow, dumped on his hat and went out on to the porch where Martin stopped him.

'Paw, he's right, it'd be a hell of a life for Nan.'

The older man gazed at his son almost sorrowfully. 'Martin, there's two things I've learnt in life. One is that females get a deep itch an' nothin' will do but that they go with their man. The other one is that west of the Missouri River the world is hell on women an' horses.'

Martin heard noise down at the barn and struck out in that direction leaving his father gazing

147

after him, and thinking that having a son who was a carbon copy of his paw wasn't a good idea after all, Martin was as pig-headed as he had been when he'd been Martin's age.

Nan was making noises in the kitchen. He was turning to go inside, cast a look out and was reaching for the door when something very distant caught and held his attention. He stood very still watching. The distance was considerable but men on horseback even when they were no larger than specks, were distinctly different when moving from other critters.

At the distance the riders were discernible it would be a long time before they reached the yard. Amos went down to the barn where Elijah's hired men were dunging out horse stalls in total silence, their faces closed down around their thoughts.

There was no sign of Martin but as the old man entered the barn his eldest son came in from out back. He'd been leaning on corral stringers watching horses eat – and thinking.

The old man's words stopped all three of them in their tracks. 'Riders comin' from the east.'

They stood in the front barn opening silent and squinty-eyed. The riders Amos had seen had picked up their gait. They were now clearly visible, but except for the sun's brilliance details would not have been clear, even then the distance continued to obscure such things as faces.

At the house Castle and Nan were finishing the dishes while he entreated her not to ride away with him. He pointed out all the perils and disadvantages. She worked and said nothing until he had exhausted all his arguments, then she turned and spoke.

'Last night … You weren't trifling?'

'No.'

'Neither was I. Al, no matter what, when two people care a lot, one abandoning the other one makes the one left behind die a little every day. I don't care about moving a lot, about looking over our shoulders. Do you understand?'

He put aside the drying cloth, reached, pulled her close and held her without speaking until she raised her face. Outside, that was the moment her father had his hand on the door to enter. He was distracted or he would have walked in on something that would have shocked him down to his boots. It wasn't their first kiss but it was their most passionately yearning one. When Nan stepped back without lowering her eyes, all Castle's resolve dissolved. He said, 'Tonight, then.'

She gazed at him before she said, 'Al, you meant those things you said last night, didn't you?'

He reached again and although she came close he could sense a faint hesitation or reluctance. He held her tighter. 'I don't want to leave you – ever. It's just that in Montana I'm an outlaw, a horse thief. You've got life ahead of you, maybe someday with a man who don't have a dodger out on him.'

She roughly pushed clear. 'I don't care about the dodger! I told you that last night … Al; if you leave me I'll be lost. I told you last night, since down where you shot the Gila monster; I guess before that, you were all I thought about, all I wanted.'

He watched her expression change as she spoke. He'd known a few women, not many, never one like Nan Humphrey. He only understood love from instinct. He smiled at her. 'Tonight, the two of us, and together from then on no matter what happens or who puts troubles in our path.'

'Do you honestly love me, Al? I'm not pretty. I'm not even very feminine. I've known that since I had pigtails.'

He replied softly. 'Let me tell you something, Nan Humphrey: The first time I saw you in the yard ... Morris an' Avery told me to be careful of you because you're strong an' knocked some feller down who tried to kiss you. When I was tryin' to get out of the country, I thought of you – it was like leavin' a part of me back in the Campton country.'

'I'm not pretty, Al.'

That statement was beginning to annoy him. He took both her hands in his. 'You *are* pretty. You're one hell of a female-woman ... The first town we come to that's got a preacher we'll get married, and maybe someday we can come back an' visit your paw.'

She blinked hard several times and went up against him her full length. They were standing like that when her younger brother burst in – and stopped as though he'd run into a stone wall.

Castle released her. Nan turned, saw who it was, her favourite brother, and smiled at him. She did not get a chance to speak. Her brother ran his words together when he said, 'Riders comin' from the east!'

Al rolled down the sleeves he'd rolled up to help clean up the kitchen. He was moving past her when Nan said, 'Stay inside. Pete, call to Paw and the others. We got to all be together when they get here. Inside forted up.'

Pete went only as far as the porch and called to the men at the barn. Avery and Morris started for the house immediately. Amos and his eldest boy remained in the barn doorway like twin statues. Pete called more insistently to them. Amos muttered something to Martin as he struck out toward the house. Martin trailed him by a yard or two, watching the oncoming riders as he walked along.

Nan had rounded up all the weapons throughout the house. When she handed her father his favourite long-barrelled Winchester, he smiled at her. She was too busy to smile back.

In the back room old Elijah was squawking like a magpie. No one heeded that until they all had either carbines or rifles, then Amos went down the dingy hallway to Elijah's room.

Martin went to a window to peer out. Pete was slyly grinning. When he had a chance he called his sister 'General Nan,' which brought rueful grins from Avery and Morris. Al Castle grinned too, but he winked and she winked back.

Martin spoke without turning away from the window. 'There's only three of 'em.' He sounded puzzled. When he finally faced into the room he was faintly frowning until Al Castle said, 'Palaver, maybe, not fight – unless they got friends sneakin' in from out back.'

Martin jerked his head. Pete immediately turned toward the back of the house. Morris was eyeing that whiskey bottle on the little table where Amos had left it the previous night. Avery growled at him. 'Leave it be! I don't cotton to the notion of someone behind me with a loaded gun who's half full of firewater.'

Morris threw a resentful scowl at Avery but did not look at the bottle again.

Pete returned from the back of the house looking wide-eyed at Martin. 'No sign of riders in back, nor to the east or west as near as I could see ... Martin?'

'What.'

'If there's only three of them, they aren't going to make a fight.'

Castle interrupted the two-way conversation. 'Talk, gents. They're goin' to talk you into handin' me over. That's my guess.'

Martin growled his comment to that. 'Then they made a long ride for nothin'. We got nothin' to tell 'em but to get their butts off our land.'

Nan went over and brushed her oldest brother lightly with one hand. She didn't speak but he turned, gazed a long moment at her, then said, 'Paw told me just before we left the barn you'n Castle are bounden. Well; that makes Al Castle part of the family, don't it?'

Nan blinked and turned away as Amos came from the back of the house and asked Martin what he could see. When he told the old man it was only three horsemen, Amos strode to the window to verify this for himself, then leaned aside his Winchester rifle. 'That's Tom Waters in the middle. The other two are Forrest Morgan an' Len Cunningham.' He turned a puzzled face to Martin. Before the old man spoke Martin said, 'Palaver so's we'll hand over Al Castle.'

The old man faced the window again and was silent. They were all silent, the riders were entering the yard past several dowdy old cottonwood trees. Even though Amos blocked part of the window the others could see and recognise the riders.

Elijah bellowed from the back of the house. His words weren't entirely understandable but his insistence was. Nan left the parlour.

Elijah was again trying to get into his britches, but his right leg wouldn't cooperate and his right arm wouldn't either. Nan did as she'd done before after leaning aside her weapon, she grabbed Elijah from behind, lifted him and dropped him atop the bed, yanked off the one trouser leg he'd gotten a foot into and levelled a stiff finger. 'Do you recollect what I told you over at your place? I'll strip you naked, carry you outside an' leave you on the porch. Tom Waters, Cunningham an' Forrest Morgan are out there … You want to try gettin' out of bed again?'

Elijah scrabbled with both hands to cover himself with the quilts as he said, 'What do they want?'

'Al Castle. There wouldn't be no other reason for them to come out here, just three of them.'

'*Castle!*' the old man exclaimed. As before, when he was upset or angry he did not slur words. 'Listen to me, girl. This is my fight. I'm the one who kept him on, kept him in the country.'

The old man abruptly stopped ranting. The look on Nan's face was an expression he hadn't seen on a woman's face since many, many years before when his wife had shone the same quiet radiance.

He said, 'Like I told you, girl, I'll give you land an' the cattle to get the pair of you started.'

She went to bedside, leaned and kissed him, then left the room. Elijah was frozen for a full minute then said, 'Son of a bitch? By golly she's plumb taken with him.'

Out front the three horsemen swung off and tied up at the barn, then walked purposefully in the direction of the main-house. They were solemn, did not speak among themselves, and moved without haste. Martin and Al Castle, watching from the window, were both impressed with their solemnity. Martin said, 'There's somethin' wrong.'

Amos stepped outside without his Winchester. He had his holstered sidearm when he nodded and the three visitors smiled back. Amos waited until they were on the porch. He blocked the front door and gestured toward chairs.

None of them sat. Cunningham and Morgan did not look at Amos, they gazed elsewhere while the lawman said, 'You got Al Castle inside?'

Amos nodded without speaking.

'Well,' the marshal said, 'we'd like to have him out here.'

This time Amos spoke. 'Not on your life, Tom. If you try to take him you're likely to get hurt. The boys an' Elijah's two riders are inside. We been expecting trouble. We're ready for it.'

Marshal Waters gazed steadily at the older man. 'If I'd come for trouble, Amos, I'd have brought a posse.'

'Then what did you come for?'

'To tell you'n Castle somethin' that might interest you. You want to get him?'

Amos shifted his stance, considered the marshal's companions, both of whom had been breathing fire in town. It was Len Cunningham who spoke next. 'We're not goin' to try'n take him, but he'd ought to be out here. This won't take long, Amos, an' you got my word we're not here for trouble.'

Amos reached behind to open the door as he looked at Cunningham. His expression showed what he was thinking – if they tried to arrest Al Castle on his porch they'd regret it as long as they lived.

He leaned and called into the parlour. 'Al; mind steppin' out here?'

Nan reached for Castle's arm but he was already moving. She did not make contact. When Castle passed through the door to the porch he left the door ajar.

Tom Waters considered Castle. 'Bishop an' Morrison got hung last night. Tell him, Len.'

Cunningham, who had been one of those adamant about lynching Castle with the other two, would not meet Castle's gaze. He was as uncomfortable as he'd ever been in his life. In fact he wouldn't have been on the porch if Marshal Waters hadn't threatened to jail him for murder.

'Morrison,' he said gruffly, 'told us the names of them two fellers you shot at Corral Canyon. Mullins and Spence.' Cunningham hesitated until Tom Waters turned scowling. 'Morrison told us they never seen you before in their lives until they come to town. They said him an' Bishop was fixin' to join the other two and drive the cattle north when the noise in town died down.'

Cunningham was staring at the wall. Forrest Morgan added a little more. 'Bishop was still cussin' us when the rope cut his wind off, but Morrison was talkin' a blue streak and ended up blubberin' like a baby when he was set on a horse, hands tied in back an' the rope was around his neck ... Tom said we had to come out here and set the record straight. You wasn't a rustler.'

Someone inside the house made a sobbing, rough laugh. It wasn't a man's voice.

Morgan and Cunningham stood like mutes until the marshal poked each one of them. 'The rest of it!'

It was easier for Morgan to apologise than it was for Len Cunningham, but they both did it. Tom Waters held out his hand to Al Castle. 'I didn't believe it. I had a hunch last night, I went out to see Forrest Morgan and Len Cunningham. I knew they'd been part of the lynch crowd. It took a little persuasion but they told me what Morrison had said.' Waters took back his hand. 'It was a real close call. If Morrison hadn't tried to trade the truth for his life, that was enough. But it had to come from Morrison or Bishop. You understand?'

Castle nodded.

Amos relaxed. Behind him in the doorway his eldest son filled the opening. He wasn't as relieved as Al Castle was. Nor was he as willing to feel grateful for what the town marshal had done. He shouldered around his father, speared Len Cunningham with a contemptuous look as he said, 'You know, Len, since I can remember you been a nervous, damned fool who went off half cocked. If I was Al I'd take you two down to the barn one at a time and overhaul you real good.'

Amos growled. 'That's enough, Martin. You gents care to come inside an' have somethin' to eat with us?'

Before Cunningham, Morgan or the town marshal could reply Nan appeared in the doorway. 'Maybe someone can shoot a crow for Len and Forrest. That's all they'll get if I have to cook it.'

Amos made a rattling sigh before addressing the lawman. 'Maybe you gents just better ride on back.'

As the trio from Campton went down to get astride and ride easterly with the sun in their faces, Avery, Morris, the three Humphrey men and Nan Humphrey stood on the porch watching them depart.

Nan grabbed Al's arm, her eyes brilliant with relief. Amos frowned at his daughter's forwardness, herded his sons inside and closed the door.

Al pulled Nan close, held her so tightly he could feel the echoes of her heartbeat. Neither of them said a word until Nan pushed free as she spoke. 'Come inside with me. I want you to hear what old Elijah told me.'

They passed through the parlour. In the kitchen Amos and his sons were sitting at the table sharing a bottle of pop skull, they saw Nan pulling Al along by the hand but pretended they hadn't seen them.

Elijah's colour was good and his eyes were bright when he saw his visitors. He wanted to know about the men from Campton. Nan told him.

Elijah slapped his quilts with the one hand that he could rely on to do what it was told.

'I knew it. It couldn't end no other way. Nan, he's a good man – don't argue – I been readin' humanity like a book for more'n sixty-five years ... Boy, I told her I'd deed you several thousand acres and give you the seed stock to get started with.'

Al Castle saw the misty eyes of the woman whose hand he was holding. He freed himself, went to bedside and leaned to offer a hand. Before he could get it raised Elijah pulled violently away and said, 'Don't you dare. I've shot men for less. A handshake will do just fine.'

Castle twisted to put a puzzled look in Nan's direction. She didn't explain, she broke into laughter.